Encore

Writers

Edited By
Diana Kathryn Plopa

Grey Wolfe Publishing, LLC
PO Box 1088
Birmingham, Michigan 48009
www.GreyWolfePublishing.com

© 2015 Grey Wolfe Publishing, LLC
Published by Grey Wolfe Publishing, LLC
www.GreyWolfePublishing.com
All Rights Reserved

ISBN: 978-1628281262

Library of Congress Control Number: 2015951653

Encore Writers

An Anthology of the Writers of NEXT
A 50+ Population Community Center

Edited by Diana Kathryn Plopa

A Writer or an Author?
That is the question.

Many have asked, "Am I a Writer or an Author? And, what's the difference?" This book is an exploration of that contemplation.

Many who write do it only for themselves or for their closest companions. Secretly sometimes, they write in journals, sequestered computer files, or in loose-leaf notebooks, recording their thoughts, ideas, poetry, stories of fantasy and histories. They write not for the accolades of publication, but as a way to purge the grey matter of their minds. They are Writers. They will probably always write.

Many who write also publish. They want to share what they write with the world... financial gain is usually ancillary. The point in publishing is to reach out, become heard, and leave a lasting legacy. They are Authors. And, they too, will probably always write.

It's important to understand that the distinction of the two labels is not a judgment. It's not about expressing success, or inadequacy. It's merely a word one uses to simplify what could become a complex explanation.

We are all Writers. And now, with this anthology, we are all Authors, too. Tomorrow, we will be Writers again; because if you write, you know; the Celebration of the Written Word is never ending.

Table of Contents

1.

A Change in World View
Sara Burnside

I have become an isolationist. Except for providing support and help for countries that have suffered natural disasters or are suffering from famine, I believe the United States should not interfere with political or revolutionary issues within other nations. Trying to force countries to embrace a democracy or rid them of alien forces within their borders is simply not in the best interest of our country. We Americans fought our own battles to become free and to develop our own version of democracy. Besides, how successful have we been in sending military resources or actually intervening with our soldiers? Korea, Vietnam, Iraq, Afghanistan, come to mind. Often, our good intentions have led to unintended consequences.

I find it immoral to send pilotless drones that may or may not hit their intended target, but too often kill innocent people. Do we really think we are going to kill off all terrorists in the world or those who would wish us ill? And after our pre-emptive strike against Iraq, foreign leaders have every right to mistrust us. We have an arsenal of nuclear weapons and are at the ready to invade any country we wish, with or without justification. Isn't it understandable or even inevitable that other nations want to build up their own defenses?

America's best defense against attack from other nations is to secure our own borders. 9/11 happened because our FBI and CIA were not sharing intelligence and not following up on legitimate information. We Americans must be ever-vigilant in this dangerous world against any potential threat to our way of life. With a more humanitarian view and less interfering approach, we might even gain a more positive regard abroad.

NOTE: Aging has led me toward a more peaceful nation and world view.

2.
A Fascination
Diana Kathryn Plopa

Treading softly upon the floor
Aiming carefully but missing my mark
The boards creek and you awaken

Your long slender body arches upward as your
Wondrous eyes pierce my soul... The walls around us echo
The silence of the many before us
Who have been as we are now... Helpless and lost... Drowning
In a sea of expectation

Several minutes pass as we stand together
Though we never touch... Locked in our gaze
Is what comes next

I move a moment closer, yet once again, Caught in my tracks
A light shines from someplace deep inside you
It begs me to come closer... But warns of hidden dangers
Within your power

Afraid... I turn to go
For I am uncertain of what you could unlock in me

You catch me again
Your eyes won't release me... Your soul won't release me
Your power holds me strong... Drawing me again to you
A breeze floats through the room... Yet all is still
The silence is so deafening
The light in you grows stronger... I am powerless against it

You bring me in closer... Deeper into that part of you
Where you hide your secrets... And your strengths

Our souls collide in a cascade of colors
Melting together in a timeless dance of eternal oneness
Together we create a single spark
The universe vibrates with exhilaration

As our flame ignites
We realize now... We are one... At least in this way... Forever

A fascination forged in steel
And hardened through... Something... Encapsulated in us

At last you relinquish your hold
And I slip away into the darkness... Dew falls on my face
A warm wind blows through my heart
And I recall the words... Once released but never forgotten
The night wraps around me... Like too many old movies
I stroll the old places... And think of you

3.
A Sore Loser
Diana Kathryn Plopa

She was everything her mother had told her not to be, and still, it hadn't made a difference. Raised in a highly conservative family with the tumult of propriety everywhere she turned, it was difficult to win. She dressed well, had impeccable manners, and a dowry large enough to capture preeminent suitors... and still, it wasn't enough. She wanted something more, something different.

One day, he came to her door, roses in one hand, and a proposal of marriage in the other. Of course, her parents approved; he was from good stock and had a bank balance that mirrored his social standing. He was the finest champagne of men, oozing refinement and promising a life of forever bliss. In her soul, she knew it was a scam, but went along anyway; accepting the loss of any individuality she may have attained had she played the game differently.

Three years later, they had two delightful children, and a nanny to care for them. She pranced the social scene unencumbered by poverty or guilt, making good use of charity to fill her lost evenings. He immersed himself in his work and was rarely present – physically, emotionally, spiritually, sexually or in nearly every other way – except financially. It's what kept her content. And still, it wasn't enough. She wanted something more, something different. She'd lost the teenage fantasy of her white knight; and she had accepted that loss with the daily immersion of false prophets who regaled her with the hint of emancipation through prayer, wine, and tolerance. The effect was only slightly comforting.

Twenty years passed. The children had grown and moved on to take up residence in the finest Universities of Europe, chasing dreams and catching rainbows. Each found a path of least resistance, which also provided for some modicum of joy and success. They weren't yet satisfied – but they were working at it, fervently. She envied their opportunity and courage. She'd lost all of that with the acceptance of a rose on the veranda of a summer afternoon.

She remained at home, fighting off the jealousies of women who floated ghost-like through her marriage; never truly discovering *her* path of least resistance. Agitation and quiet rage, she came to understand, could not compete with the undulation of apathy or the small flame of happiness she dared to reach for; the singe of its heat eluding her. She wanted nothing more. She'd lost the spark.

When he died tragically, on a ferry while commuting home from his latest lover's chateau, of a brain aneurysm, she did not weep for him. Why should she? She'd lost the continuance she'd been dependent on for thirty years, and she was irritated that he'd left her the burden of their vast estate. There were lawyers to handle the delicate complications, of course; but she was saddled with the annoyances of the daily ills of maintenance. She'd lost the recumbent lifestyle to which she had become accustomed. She was on her feet now, more than was comfortable; a telephone relentlessly dangling within reach as she was forced to make decisions, choose paths that could never relinquish resistance, and parent her grown children a continent away.

She resented all he had left her. She resented all he had done to keep her placid over the decades they'd been together. She resented the plans she was now forced to make in order to preserve her children's entitlement program. She'd never wanted any of this. Now that she'd lost the key to her self-loathing with no target of amiable anxiety, she resented herself.

The housekeeper found her a month after his death, her naked body draped with the jewels of his false remorse; her head lying on a pillow of the pages of his portfolio, stained with the blood of her awareness. She'd left the world lost in a sea of heaving self-doubt. She'd had it all, she'd lost nothing tangible, only the love she never possessed; and yet, she rallied against her privilege and resented the moment he'd left her with responsibility.

She hadn't coped with losing well.

4.
A Tribute To My Mother
On Mother's Day
Niru Prasad

My mother was the focal point of my life during early childhood. Unfortunately, my seven siblings and I lost our mother when I was very young. By the grace of God, all of us did very well in life; our parents nurtured us with a foundation of good morals and family values, and emphasized the value of education.

I attribute my success in life to the moral, intellectual, and physical education I received from my mother. There are a few pieces of advice given by her when I was growing that have lingered with me forever. I'd like to share this with my children, and I would now like to share it with you:

1) Education is the most valuable gift in life. In order to build your career, it is very important to stay focused; set up your goals and stick with them.

2) Help others with compassion, kindness, and gentleness.

3) Always count your blessings and remember that God is there to help you during the difficult days in life.

4) Never compare yourself to others.

5) Remember to walk straight with your head up to the sunshine; then you will never see your shadow behind you.

6) Do not dwell on the past. The future is not ours to say, but we can look optimistically towards it.

7) Trust in God and give thanks to Him every day.

8) Understand that a wonderful day in life is another great gift we are blessed with daily.

9) Live and enjoy every single day of your life.

Mother's Day is the perfect day to celebrate the joy of having your mother and thanking her for everything she has done for you throughout your life.

5.
A Voice in the Wilderness
Al Rosie

Two facts became evident early in my Gong Show Career:

1. If it ain't risqué, it just won't play.

2. The younger generation didn't dig my stuff.

My fourth appearance was at the Underground in Ypsilanti. This was a popular hangout for students from Eastern Michigan University—aka Michigan Normal—when my great-grandmother graduated in its first class. Initially, I drove right past the place—it actually was underground. I reached the outskirts of Ann Arbor before I realized I had gone too far, but retraced my route and still arrived with time to spare. I never wanted to keep my public waiting.

Only six members of Wally's gang showed up, and as usual, I was spotted second on the bill. Because of the shortage of competitors, I surmised the judges were asked to go easy on the gong so the performers could do a second number. I opened with my old reliable "The Chauvinist Cowboy" which was risqué enough to survive a number of shows. For the only time in my career, I was asked to do an encore. This time I tried a more meaningful song with a slower tempo, but Red Jamison, a sportscaster for Channel 2, who was one of the judges, gonged me as soon as the guaranteed forty seconds had elapsed. While the clanging was still ringing in my ears, a female voice in the audience piped up, "I thought he was funny!" Bless her heart! I never saw her face, but the thought that one person appreciated what I was trying to do set the tone for my entire showbiz career. After that, rejection never bothered me and

I was able to deal with my numerous failures with comparative grace.

My boyhood idol, Dick Wakefield of the Detroit Tigers, was another of the judges and I walked over and got his autograph before I left the stage. I had come up from Monterey to see him play with the Oakland Seals when I was studying at the Army Language School in 1951. The thought of having gonged me must have preyed on Red Jamison's mind because he committed suicide within two years (actually he was depressed after being fired from a couple of jobs and divorced by his wife).

Another disaster with the college crowd came at Ma Bell's in Belleville. The feature of this venue was a phone on every table so people who thought you looked hot could ring you up and get acquainted. Nobody called me all evening. Here's the song I tried that night "Don't You Wish You Could Gong Jimmy Carter". As usual, I got gonged about half way through it—the judge must have been a Democrat. Several months later, I tried the same song at Gino's Surf over on Lake St. Clair and judge Bill Anderson, a country music DJ, contributed my first TEN saying he didn't like Ted Kennedy either. I'm not saying I sewed up Michigan's electoral votes for Reagan that year, but you can draw your own conclusions.

6.

An Autumn Evening's Respite
Susanne Sack

My name is "Cheeta Marie". The thick forest leaves are beginning to change. I see the deer poke their heads very carefully through the underbrush. Their lovely bright tan color is modifying to help them hide from their predators. If only they would just stay in one position while I paint them. They move and of course, that makes my portrait more natural. The photo I am taking will give me the facts. The moving reality in the long shadowed light of the early morning makes my heart sing. The conditions will lend to my work, joy and more excitement with each movement of the pencil and each brush stroke.

I counted the number of babies. There were thirty fawns born in the early spring and there are thirty young deer in the Fall. Ten adult doe and sixteen yearling doe remain. The male yearlings add up to nine. There were five bucks but two were killed during the rut. Across the Highway, on the private school property and beyond are living another extended family of deer about the same in number. The small animals in the neighborhood that are compatible with the deer are groundhogs, rabbits, neutered feral cats, squirrels, rats, mice, moles, voles and others under the ground.

The bird population has diminished to leave only a few that live high in trees, or rest in chimneys. Homes are specially built to retain and control the bird population. All decks and patio are fenced with twelve-foot high chain link with screening on the inside. Some have a ceiling screen with small entrances for the birds to enter and feed. Birds which nest low have disappeared or relocated. On my roof, the chimney has been reinforced and capped so the Sparrows can have their homes and we have a chimney that works. The eaves are safe places for the young and fledgling house finches.

I really miss the birds of color and song who no longer entertain us. Suddenly I see a friend sitting atop one of the shorter trees. He is red, black and white; bigger than a robin. We haven't seen robins for several years, at least a decade. They always chose low places for their nests. This fellow is grosbeak just a great big robin with brighter colors. The hawks have eliminated most of the Grosbeaks in our area. The only birds we now see are in the higher locations that hide from the many birds of prey that come each late afternoon. The nighthawks still hunt in the dark.

After a day of painting I see that the darkening indigo sky is so beautiful, I cannot resist designing a canvas. My color memory is such that I can use the pencil to sketch what I want to paint. Tonight will be soon enough to use the colors. I watch the nighthawks with their wings outstretched circling their prey. They take a deep dive toward the small animals. A squeal, almost a scream tells me it's time to fold up my easel, pack up my paints, and enter the gate on my patio. I lock it up for the night. With the shortening days, I am leaving earlier each night.

Inside my seventy-five-year-old colonial home, I feel safe and snug. I lower the wooden exterior blinds with the electrical control.
It isn't safe to leave them up even in pleasant weather. It would be good to have a breeze in the house.

Suddenly I hear a thump, then another and another against the roof and the wooden blinds. The screaming of the night animals and their prey begins. That's when I press the key to the ocean sounds on my house sound system. Some neighbors keep their music on all night. When dawn comes, the quiet comes for another day until the red-tails and Turkey Buzzards begin the hunt in the late afternoon.

****

I have been painting since I was very young. I had art lessons outside of school since I was eleven. I have illustrated for several children's science books. My work has appeared in nature magazines, and I had a show of my work several times in different cities. In general, I love nature and animals. I am glad I can live my dream.

Today is another kind of day. I will not be able to paint outdoors today. The Cat is back. She has had her two baby cubs and they are not with her. She would be an excellent subject for my next article. The N.E.T., the government's control agency, has been watching her to make sure no-one harms her or her two cubs. My painting can be done anywhere where there is good light and a good atmosphere. Not too humid, not too dry so the paint doesn't dry too fast, or too slow. I prefer oil paints even though they are much harder to purchase. Most painters are using water colors. Oil is increasingly harder to use for any purposes. It is considered dangerous. I actually get my oil paints from people who have connections. I need to be careful or I may be sued or even arrested.

Today I won't be painting outdoors. Our favorite wild cat has presented her greeting. She normally warns that she has her cubs with her. All the lowest wildlife either go underground or inside a tree, or disguise themselves as best they are able. She likes people and appreciates the attention as she proudly shows off her babies. Then she hunts for supper for her growing boys. Most people leave a steak or two for her, just to keep her friendly and to protect the local wildlife. The neighborhood families, of which there are fewer and fewer, are very protective of their children and insist they stay in after six o'clock at night. There is a curfew for all people after seven o'clock pm when the days get shorter, and nine o'clock in the summer. The Coyotes come through looking for leftovers later in the evening, following the cat and her babies.

I am getting tired and don't think I will paint until morning. But, at around a quarter past nine, I receive a call from a neighbor looking for a dog that got out before curfew. The woman is frantic and very upset, blaming her husband for opening the door too wide and letting the dog out.

"Mary, I will keep a look-out in the woods as long as I can, but it is getting dark." I put down the phone and look out my dining room window. I don't see anything but shadows at this time of night.

A while later, as I am getting ready for bed, I hear a scream and a yip from the back of my house. A police siren sounds and in a few minutes well padded, armed police officers race down our steps in back carrying a giant net and hook.

A black panther is living in the next town and every now and then he runs out of meat from the neighbors. He is looking for leftovers from the cat's dinner in our woods. The last time he visited he caught a child who had run away into the woods. The kid had a gun and was going to protect himself from the animals. The Panther, being a wild animal, pounced on the kid when he was sleeping inside a hollow log. The panther dragged him out by his leg. The police barely got there in time to sedate the animal. The kid needed sedating and a physician's care. He never tried that trick again. The rest of the neighborhood kids learned a lesson from that experience. But tonight, the panther is gathered up and transported to his sector of the community. The lost dog was not lost at all but had run back in the house before anyone closed the door and was hiding under the bed. Most domestic animals are too smart to go out.

The net and hook is not for the panther this time. A Coyote is caught in a neighbor's fence and is whooping it up, crying for help. He is tearing up his leg trying to free himself. Eventually, the poor animal is given first aid for his injuries and released into the woods again. I hope there is a quiet night tonight. I want to paint, close my shutters and turn on my quiet music.

First I call my daughter to see how she is doing in her southern town. They have more trouble with raccoons and buzzards than we do in the north. "Mother, will you pray for our neighborhood. We are having trouble with poachers snaring our wildlife and selling them on the black market to other countries who have not joined the World Organization for the Prevention of Cruelty of Animals." W.S.P.C.

"Oh, dear that will ruin the balance of nature for us," I reply. "I think we need stricter laws for such behavior."

Morning is here after a short night of painting. I gave up about three o'clock in the morning 3:00 am and fell asleep in my studio. Today I will leave the compound and pick up a bus to the city. The City Market has specials on bird seed and beef for the woods. I have planted native plants from the market that supply the birds with the food in the wooded area behind my home. Today is a beautiful day for being outdoors. The bus is almost empty. I talk to the driver who seems a bit quiet, almost morose today. "Not many aboard today!" I say.

"No, fortunately." the driver replies."

"Why is that?" I return.

"What does that mean?" he retorts.

"It's such a beautiful day," I say. "Is it?" I'm not interested in continuing the conversation.

"Soon another passenger boards the bus. "I really don't know why I continue going to the market since I am hearing rumors that it is increasingly more dangerous to do so," the woman remarks.

"How can it be dangerous in the daytime?" I ask.

"Rumor has it they are letting the Panthers roam during the day." she replies.

"I'm certainly glad it is only a rumor," I say.

She shakes her head and remains silent the rest of the twelve-mile ride to the market.

We arrive and I alight from the bus and search for places to set up my easel. I paint for a while. It is enjoyable to capture the shoppers at the market. I don't see too many people in one place very often. The crowds are fun to paint, pushing each other, arguing about who gets the sale item. The variety of styles of clothing pleases the color expression in me. After I pack up my paints and easel, I shop a while and buy some bread and cheese for lunch. I find a place to eat under a roof with picnic tables. I talk with the shopper near me. He is busy finding food for the bear that lives in his part of town along with two cubs. Lastly, I enjoy some wine. I buy my beef and some small plants for the woods.

I board the bus. Quite a few people return with me. I talk to the woman next to me. "What a pleasant day. I hardly ever get out to shop and enjoy the market." She sadly speaks, "I heard they are closing it next week."

"Closing what?" I ask with surprise.

"The Market is closing. Sale of all meat will be by the Web from now on."

It is difficult carrying the meat unless you disguise the meat smell with Coverscent. Usually, very few people are on the bus. Today the bus is so strong with the odor that it almost makes me sick. The chrysanthemums purchased at the market help me to get home without stopping somewhere to recover. Holding the beautiful fall roses to my nose I try to substitute the smell of the Coverscent but the effort is in vain. I jump out of the bus and begin the fairly short walk home. It is relatively quiet. Suddenly I see a dark shadow pass me. "Oh, no, it's the panther with his long tongue hanging out and saliva dripping off the sides of his jowls."

Suddenly he begins to circle the area in which I am walking. I am terrified and he can smell the fear. I blow my whistle, but he doesn't let the discomfort bother him. I keep blowing, but he circles me until I run out of air to blow. Fear grips my soul and body. I lie down and submit myself to the superiority of the black devil. He is taking my package but without leaving my side, he tears apart the package. He leaves the package of meat and begins to sniff my feet, legs trunk and neck. "Why are you doing this?" He roars as he tears at my shoulder. The pain sears and I cannot move, nor speak, nor even scream. My last memory is two yellow eyes staring into mine.

Today I am in a hospice for terminally ill patients. They could not save my body, but my brain is hooked up to equipment to keep me alive so they can study my brain. The study, I heard from the resident scientist's discussion today, is aimed toward training humans to submit to animal aggression. Only people who leave their compounds will be used as food for the animals. This is a very carefully guarded secret program. Many are complaining about the slaughter of cattle and there is a fear of uprising from the militant fundamentalist animal worshipers. A few who leave the compound will be attacked methodically by the "Black Panther" king of the urban beasts for the purpose of sacrificing to the "Holy Animals" throughout the city.

I am submitting to the inevitable and trying to enjoy my final days which are soon to end. The light is dimming and I am losing consciousness. *Oh! if only I could warn them!* My tears are not forthcoming. My tears are not warning anyone. *Goodbye!*

7.
Anger and Grief
Diana Kathryn Plopa

"Anger suffers as grief withdraws." At least that's what my shrink told me as I clutched the pillow to my chest, watching the heartless snow fall upon his Cambridge window pane. He said, "Don't worry Amy, as your grief goes away, so will your anger; for the two cannot live without each other. They feed on each other. Grief soothes anger. Anger feeds grief. When you can bring yourself to let go of one, the other will also disappear. It's the simple nature of things."

As I wrote the check and dropped it in the competent hands of his secretary, I left that session with a new appreciation for life, death, anger, grief, and the stupidity of psychoanalysis.

Simply put, my Harvard educated, psych-babble wielding, one-hundred-dollar-per-hour egomaniac analyst was wrong. Good old doctor What's It got it wrong. After the few brief months of the all-consuming grief of my mother's passing subsided, the anger remained... and in full force; albeit just under the surface of my daily life; irritating every thought, every decision, every joy.

Each day, I recalled the fact that my mother, with whom I had parted company on less-than-stellar terms, was no longer in my life. And I was still angry about the fact. I was angry that our last conversation together was not a pleasant one; and angry that she had refused to do anything to improve her situation in life... for years.

As I walked the snow-covered streets from the T-station back to my apartment on Boylston Street, I rehashed the frustration, reinvigorating the anger with each sloshing step of boot against icy pavement. My mother had spent the last five years self-medicating and ignoring the advice of doctors; claiming, "They don't really know what they're talking about and clearly, I know my body much better than they do. After all, I live with it every day."

Our heated phone call ended with my telling her, "After four years of medical school, four years of residency, and who knows how many years in practice affiliated with a top-rated hospital, you're going to question your cardiologist?"

She said, "I don't want to discuss this anymore." And there was silence on the line. She had hung up on her daughter. The whole thing was nuts! And so, without much fanfare, she died three weeks later. She had a heart attack on Easter morning. I didn't expect her resurrection, even though she had been baptized not many years before in the very same waters that John had dunked Jesus.

As the grief withdrew, the anger swelled within me, tainting my memory of her and the childhood we shared. The anger that lingered made me question the happy memories I had of her... made me question my relationship with her... made me question – albeit briefly – my actions as a mother. I had vowed not to follow in her negative footsteps, and only resole the positive steps. Would I do that? The anger of her passing made me question far too much. And the grief no longer consoles.

When I brought this inconsistency to the attention of dear Dr. What's It, all he could say was, "Everyone grieves differently, Amy. Your process is unlike anyone else's."

Then why, I thought, am I paying you ridiculous amounts of money each month to convince me there are rules about these things, and answers easily found if I sacrifice my most conflicting thoughts on your couch of absolution? That was the last time Dr. What's It and I spent any time together. I don't miss him, and I doubt he misses me.

It's been over a year now, and I've made peace with my anger... dislodged my grief... and subsisted on the understanding that we all do the best we can in this world... to get by. And for those of us who don't try, well, they get what they get; and we, sooner or later, become comfortable with our discomfort when reflecting on the aftermath.

8.

Bigamy

Al Rosie

He was a man of many wives and many names. Born in Glasgow, Scotland, in 1840, he was christened Patrick Henry O'Hanlon. Ten-year-old Patrick immigrated with his family to Toledo, Ohio, in 1850.

"No Irish Need Apply" was a popular song of the era and Thomas O'Hanlon apparently felt it applied to him, because he dropped the initial "O" from the family name shortly after his arrival in the USA. Young Patrick took it a step further by dropping his given name "Patrick" before he reached adulthood.

In 1863 young Hanlon married Anna Fisher, the daughter of a well-to-do Ohio millwright. A photograph of the couple reveals a scrawny looking lad alongside a woman who might charitably described as "plain" who outweighed him by a good sixty pounds.

Hannibal Hamlin was Vice President of the United States at the time and Hanlon thought he might be more readily accepted into the all-German 107th Ohio Infantry Volunteers by borrowing the Vice President's name, so he signed up as Henry Hamlin. The 107th fought at Gettysburg and perhaps Hamlin was wounded in the battle since his next assignment was on Johnson's Island, Ohio, where Confederate officers were imprisoned.

Possibly the proximity to southern gentlemen triggered a desire to become one himself. After the war he reverted to Hanlon again and moved his wife and two daughters to Logan, West Virginia, but in 1871 he abandoned his family and fled to Chicago where he found his true identity as Henry Floyd, the scion of

George Rogers Clark Floyd. He retained that persona until his death in 1900.

The following year he went to Bay County, Michigan, where he married Marie Leonide DuBois without bothering to divorce Anna.

Marie was a rather frail woman, although she bore a couple of children after they moved to Louisiana. However, the wanderlust struck Mr. Floyd again and he ventured off to Hillsboro, Arkansas, where he married Pauline Bussey in 1884. Marie found out where he had gone and caught up with him, but was so shocked that she was married to a bigamist that she collapsed and died on the spot. She never knew she was actually married to a trigamist— she didn't know about old faithful Anna.

At this point, Mr. Floyd decided to become the southern gentleman he had always wanted to be, so he moved with his new wife to Kentucky where he fathered two children. He became a pillar of the community and was proclaimed an honorary Kentucky colonel. He and Pauline and their children lived happily ever after.

In 1893, Floyd ventured to Chicago to attend the Columbian Exposition. He met—perhaps by chance—his original wife who had moved with her daughters to Chicago. He presented Anna with a photo of himself which shows a distinguished looking gentleman—a sharp contrast to his earlier photo. Anna made no effort to get him back, but she made sure she would be the recipient of Henry Hamlin's Civil War pension.

9.
Blond Curly Lady with the Poetic Mind
Renee Batenjany

Oh, blond lady with the curly hair, dark eyes, a non-stop spinning mind.

Oh, what rolling and rolling splendid poetic lines.

Oh Lady with the beating hearts, over heated brow, just how many errands and joyful lines have you stored in your mind.

Oh, lady with the bright, glamorous clothes, the various aged cameo collections and oh how many unique lines have you added to your clever published treasured thoughts.

Oh, blond lady with the tired Zumba legs, "is that you my funny friend disguised in an oversized hat?"

Oh, are you trying hard to hide your curlers as you complete your dancing tasks.

10.
Bonnie and Clyde
Dee Trainor

If you looked at me, I am sure you would see a sweet grandmotherly, little woman. Even in my prime at 5' 1" tall, I was never an imposing figure. You wouldn't think I had been involved with the police would you? Well, I was, in a major way!

The encounter took place one winter evening shortly after Christmas. My daughter Sharon, and her life-long friend, Peggy, both around twelve years old, and I went uptown shopping. We just got into Himeloch Department Store in Birmingham, Michigan, about fifteen minutes before closing. I do not remember why we were at Himeloch. It was an upscale store that was out of our class in those days. We were usually Kay Baums regulars, which was the top of the line for us.

We were dressed casually, in jeans, snow boots, and pea coats. Nothing special I guess, but Peggy was wearing her most prized Christmas gift—a bright red hat, sort of a beret with red matching mittens. They were what we would call "fire engine red." She was a pretty girl with long blond hair, a turned up nose, blue eyes, and naturally rosy lips. She was on the quiet side. Sharon was very pretty also, with light brown curly hair and a ready smile. She was more adventuresome and outgoing than Peggy.

When you walked through the front door at Himeloch, you were in the center of the store. To the left were cosmetics, bath powder, perfume and the like. Further to the left were gloves and purses. If you turned down that aisle, you would be in "better dresses" in the back of the store.

To the left of us, on the other side of the store, was the coat department. There were beautiful houndstooth plaid wools, a long pink leather swing coat, nay chesterfields and especially the Alpaca cashmeres. Wow! Then there were the furs. Sleek orange and black leopard coats, sheered beaver with rhinestone buttons. In many, you could see shiny gray satin linings. As we walked through we were trying to act as though we belonged there.

Then we noticed a black couple sauntering around the racks of fur coats; it caught our attention because it was unusual to see blacks in the suburbs those days. We were apparently the only customers left in the store. They were a most handsome couple but still seemed out of place. She was tall and slim wearing a purple crepe wrap-around dress caught up at the hip with a silver buckle. With her chin tipped up, she could look down over her high cheekbones and appraise the merchandise. Her companion stood patiently off to one side. He was equally as tall and slim and just as good looking. The light shade of his camel coat made his mahogany features even more striking.

The matronly saleswoman stood by and smiled with her head cocked to one side, her hands clasped together in front of her plaid pleated skirt; obviously hoping for a sale. The customer tried on a silver fox coat and preened in front of the three-way mirror. Holding the generous collar up close to her ears, she turned and slowly looked back over her shoulder and admired the image gracing the glass. Then she slipped out of the coat with her companion's help and draped it over her arm. She wanted to try on just one more coat before making a decision. This one was a gorgeous full-length black diamond mink. This image brought a gleam to her eye and caused the corners off her mouth to curl up slightly. This was the one!

We were just completing our purchase and watching the scenario about twenty feet to our right out of the corner of our eyes without trying to appear as if we were watching. (We did not want to be so provincial as to stare). Just as I zipped my purse, the sales clerk screamed. "Stop, Help, Police!" We turned to see the distinguished looking couple high-tail it out the front door. She was wearing the mink and he was carrying the fox; animal rights were not an issue in those days so it is unlikely that this was a cruelty to animals protest.

They ran straight down Bates Street, alongside Kresge's, an alley ran behind it that came out on Henrietta Street. Do not even ask me how I knew this, but I said, "I'll bet they are going through the alley – come on girls, we can head them off." To this day, I have no idea what "head them off," meant. This was either a misplaced sense of the good guys always win or I had been watching too much Dragnet (The CSI of the 60's.) The girl's eyes were as big as saucers and their mouths hung open in disbelief, but they blindly obeyed the command.

We flew down Maple; Mitzelfields, Grinnell's, Sherman Shoes all became a blur as we streaked by. We tore across at Henrietta and just as we approached the alley, unbelievably, they burst forth. We almost crashed into them; we were within four feet of the perpetrators. We stopped on a dime. We were breathless, our chests were heaving up and down, but we tried to act casual like we had been standing there for hours. Right next to us, by the curb was a black car with the doors wide open. Phase one of the "head them off" plan worked great, but now the kids were terrified and phase two of the plan was escaping me. Sharon has always had a brilliant memory for numbers even when in shock. I think even today she can recall the phone numbers of every friend she ever had.

The couple and the coats disappeared into the back seat of the car. The door slammed and the wheels squealed. Sharon said, "What should we do?"

I whispered, "Get the license plate number." Sharon tried to be casual about looking at the number and committing it to memory.

There were all kinds of commotion in town. Everyone was asking what had happened. Who did what, did they get away, etc? Of course, WE knew. We were eyewitnesses to the whole crime from the beginning to the end. Sharon was shaking and Peggy was crying. They just stood there stunned and looking at me. Now what? As Hardy would have said to Laurel, "and another fine mess you've gotten me into."

I had a cool head, my typical behavior in a crisis. (Being a mom, you get a lot of practice doing that.) Nevertheless, I must say, I was a bit shaken up myself. I said, "We'll go to the police station and report everything that happened and give them the license plate number so they can trace the criminals." We gave the police the information along with our names and addresses and an accurate account of the robbery and our quick action. The police were very grateful and appreciative of our thinking and quick wit.

As we drove home, we kept rehashing with disbelief, our experience. Then we started reviewing and analyzing they're every move. In retrospect we knew there was something suspicious about them all along! When we got home, Peggy was still crying and as she and Sharon were retelling the tale to the rest of the family, Peggy took off her treasured hat and mittens and vowed never to wear them again. She was convinced the criminals had seen her and would remember the girl in the red hat. She knew they would come back looking for her and silence her so that she could not testify against them - again, too much Dragnet.

I went back to the police station a couple of weeks later to inquire about the case. They said that thanks to our quick thinking and getting the license number of the getaway car, they were able to apprehend the criminals. They had been trying to get a break on this case for a long time and apparently, this lead to the breakup of a ring of thieves who were responsible for other robberies. (I love it when a plan comes together.)

You may wonder how I could run so fast. Remember, these are tales from the twentieth century. However, I do not think contributing to the public safety of my community has gone unnoticed. When I am out walking in the neighborhood and a police car goes by, I see them nod at me, and then I know the story of my bravery and courage are still being told: Five-foot female foils the filchers. Minute Mother out matches' mink mobsters. Terrified teen refuses to get wear red.

I never get involved with the police, ordinarily, though; unless I am getting another speeding ticket.

11.

Bytes & Bits
Jerry McKeon

My life is a digital packet
Traveling by electronic means
I zip wirelessly through the air
Obvious but never seen

My DNA is zeros and ones
An electronic folder is home
It comprises my entire life
And tracks me where I roam

Living in an electronic folder
Has it ups and downs
Every minute detail of my life
Follows me all around

12.
Channel Hopping
Al Rosie

The hand that controls the remote rules the world
Though you get your old lady's goat, you rule the world
Your terminator's in your lap
And your battlecry's "en Zap"
The hand that controls the remote rules the world.

Look, there's Vanna White, she's flippin' over "E"s
Zap, now there's a lady with a rare disease
Though you seldom know the plot
You get 'round an awful lot
The hand that controls the remote rules the world.

Commercials are a thing you can't abide
Ev'ry evening you commit commercialcide
Those poor sponsors are unwary
How you make those channels vary
The hand that controls the remote rules the world.

David Copperfield can make things disappear
If he caught your act, he'd try a new career
In your castle, he's your slave
Crook your finger—so long Dave
The hand that controls the remote rules the world.

Still, there is one show at which you always linger
Xena seems to freeze that itchy trigger finger
Waiting for that moment when
They pop out of her dress again
The hand that controls the remote rules the world.

Couch potato is the epithet you merit
Still, your searching skill would outdo any ferret
Your IQ is rather small, but you're the master of them all
The hand that controls the remote rules the world.

13.
Clara Mountain
Shelia Becker

My house was situated on the bottom of Clara Mountain. When I was there in 2006, Sean Radley took me for a most wonderful, scenic ride around the mountain. I had never been on that route before and certainly did not realize how beautiful that tour was. Many poets have been inspired to write about "Beautiful and Majestic Clara Mountain" Rising 1,486 feet above sea level, the mountain is believed to have derived its name from the flat appearance at its summit and the gradual smooth incline into the rustic valley.

I was very lucky, as it was during my stay in 2006 with my brother-in-law Tadg Driscoll, that I met Sean Radley. I went there for my brother's funeral. During my stay in Ireland, I had time on my hands because I had booked the return flight over ten days, expecting of course, I would see my brother Denny while he was still alive. In 1978, Sean Radley was one of the founding members of the Millstreet Museum Society. There is also their fairly large library, and as I had started writing my book in 2005, I was able to do a great deal of research in my family background; so I did spend every day at the library. Sean had just published "Profile of Millstreet 1880-1980.". This book is a pictorial history of Millstreet for one hundred years and has many pictures of my family and other people I grew up with.

This book explored the treasures of a bygone era. It depicted the working lives of its people, the music they played, the reality of emigration, the importance of religion, and the efforts to achieve peace during challenging times. This publication marks a significant milestone in the historic recording of Millstreet, my hometown, in such a wonderfully visual manner. It salutes its beloved people and it truly celebrates their cherished memories. Above all, "Picture Millstreet" is uplifting, enlightening and inspires a true source of hope as we approach the new millennium.

Little does any person over there realize how many times I look and re-look over the many pictures of my sisters and brothers going to school. When my own brother, Patsy, visited me from California, I could hardly get the book from him, as he would constantly say "Look at me when I was training as a mechanic at Colman's garage", he loved that book very much.

Sean Radley operated the Millstreet Museum and was a teacher at the schools for many years. He is constantly uplifted by the splendid encouragement received from a wide cross-section of local people in relation to the work being carried out at both the Museum and the Tourist information Center. It was this inspiring support which contributed to the motivation of the publication of "Picture Millstreet". Sean helped me with the final touches of my own book "My Dream from Ireland to America".

14.

College Life
Mark A. Kelly

DO I KNOW YOU?

While struggling to get through college, I went home to Cleveland for the Christmas Break. DJ Lombardo, a high school friend who was home on leave from the Air Force, called. "Mark, let's get together while we're both in town," he said with his usual enthusiasm. "I want to introduce you to this hot new bar I found. They have great live entertainment and dancing. Bring a date this Saturday night!"

"Who do you have in mind," I replied snappily. "I don't have any current dating material here in Cleveland," I pointed out to him. "Going to college in Dayton, Ohio caused my local supply to dry up. During the Christmas holidays, it's even more difficult to find available girls than during the rest of the year. The dating scene gets mighty active at this time of year."

"Try this number," he suggested. "The two of you should get along very well. She loves to dance." I wrote down the name and telephone number of the girl he suggested. Lombardo always had an extensive assortment of available girls. His taste in girls was fantastic so I didn't hesitate to make that call. With him as a referral, I had no difficulty persuading Judy to join us.

The next telephone call I received was from Frank Joyce, a friend from the University of Dayton.   He was also in Cleveland for the holidays. "What are you doing Saturday night?" he asked.

"I have a date and I'm meeting friends at this new bar."

"I thought you said you didn't know any available girls here in Cleveland. How did you find a date?"

"My friend DJ has an infinite supply of them," I bragged.

"Can he get one for me?"

"I don't know. I'll ask him." I called DJ.

"My date has a cousin that'll probably do," DJ offered. "I'll bring her along for your friend, Frank." That was mighty generous of DJ. He didn't even know Frank.

Saturday night found me driving a long distance south to pick up Judy. I took Frank along for company. Judy, Frank and I rendezvoused with DJ and his two girlfriends at his new favorite bar which, surprisingly, was located in my neighborhood. It was called *Donavan's Loop*.

The cousins were exotic looking babes. I later learned they were of Lebanese descent. Frank's date, Fay, looked vaguely familiar, but I didn't know why.

Frank tried to strike up a conversation with Sue, DJ's date, but not Fay, his date. I forgot that Frank enjoyed "bird-dogging" other guys' dates. He always seemed to think he could steal them away. Sue didn't pay any attention to Frank. When he couldn't get her attention, Frank spent most of his time drinking.

The band's lively music had DJ, Sue, Judy and me dancing most of the evening. We had a grand time. When the band took a break, the house jukebox entertained us with the popular songs of the day. A new singer by the name of Johnny Mathis seemed to be the favorite for the night with his songs *It's Not for Me to Say* and *Chances Are*. Those songs were played over and over. Fay and Sue were enamored with Johnny Mathis, which made DJ laugh. "Do you think he would make a great date?" he asked.

"Sure," they both agreed.

"You won't get far with Johnny," DJ laughed. When questioned by the girls, he said, "Johnny only likes men." I wondered why DJ thought this. The cousins were skeptical, to say the least.

"How do you know that?" they wanted to know. DJ just laughed and asked Sue to dance as the band once again took to making music. They started with *Rock Around the Clock.* Judy rocked with the best of them. They played, *Memories Are Made of This.* I whispered in Judy's ear, "We're making our own memories." She snuggled closer. A fun loving little blonde with a nice round bottom, Judy loved to dance. We did well together.

While sitting in our booth between dances, I got the impression that Fay seemed to be staring at me a lot of the time. "Do we know each other?" I asked her. "You look very familiar." She seemed extremely pleased to hear me say that. After a rundown of her genealogy, we decided that we had never met. In fact, we didn't have any friends in common other than DJ. Both she and her cousin, Sue, lived on the west side of Cleveland. "No," I had to admit, "I don't frequent your side of town."

"We go to Ursuline College in Cleveland Heights," Fay informed me. No, that didn't explain why she looked so familiar either. "Do you know anybody at John Carroll University?" she asked.

"No," I answered. That was another dead end.

My date nudged me with her bottom, which I took to mean, "That's enough time with Fay, now, how about me?"

How about her! I turned to that delightful sweetie and said, "Let's dance?" We swung away for yet another good time on the floor. The musical number was a fast tune, *Ain't That A Shame?* She could handle anything I threw at her. When I spun her out, she was like a top on a string. As I brought her back, she nestled smoothly into my arms. She really made me look good as her dancing partner. Judy wasn't only delightful on the floor but in the booth as well. She laughed a lot and carried on an engaging conversation. She seemed interested in everything I had to say.

Back in our booth, I caught Fay watching me again. I didn't spend much time looking away from Judy, but when I did, Fay would be staring at me again. I say me because it seemed very obvious. Back on the dance floor I asked Judy, "Is it my imagination or is Fay spending a lot of time staring at me?"

"Yes, she does seem preoccupied with watching you."

"Why is that?" I asked.

"She's jealous that we're having such a good time."

"She should be," I said. "You're a delightful dancer and fun to be with!"

Frank wasn't a dancer and tonight, not much of a conversationalist either. When it came time to go, Frank elected to ride home with Judy and me. Not very sociable of him since DJ had to go all the way to the west side of the city and return alone. DJ didn't seem to mind nor did Frank's date. I took Frank home before taking the long drive south to Judy's. I didn't mind the drive back alone. It was the price I paid to be alone with Judy when I dropped her at her home.

"I had a great time tonight," Judy said. "I hope to see more of you."

"I'm sorry, Judy. I'm returning to the University of Dayton tomorrow. I don't get back to Cleveland very often." I'd loved to have seen more of her. But even if I were staying in town she lived too far away. Unlike the saying, "Love knows no bounds," I was the guy who always claimed "love had a definite radius." Unfortunately,

Judy happened to be living outside of it.   Still, I'd have loved to see more of her, but my being in Dayton put her way out of that radius.

The Dating Scene

The next thing I knew, the University suggested that I take a semester off to get my act together.   I had flunked a couple of classes.   Back in Cleveland, I set a plan of action for the two most important issues in my life, a job and getting back into circulation with the dating scene.

Should I call Judy that fun-loving dancer I dated over Christmas vacation? That wasn't practical.   She lived in Brecksville, about twenty-five miles away.   Unfortunately, Judy happened to be living outside the radius of my comfort zone.

My thoughts turned to Fay, Frank Joyce's date over the Christmas break.   Fay was one of our gang of six who went dancing at DJ Lombardo's newest swinging bar *Donavan's Loop*.   DJ fixed Frank up with Fay and me with Judy.   While I danced the night away with Judy, Frank sulked in the corner ignoring Fay.   Since Fay spent a good deal of time staring at me that night, maybe it was time to find out why.   Though Fay lived on the west side of Cleveland it was only about twelve miles away.   I got her telephone number from DJ and gave Fay a call.   She was interested in seeing me again, but not on a date.

"Why don't you come to the dance this Friday night at Ursuline College?" she suggested.   That college was even closer to me than her house.   The college was in an area I knew well, *my stomping grounds.*

Friday night, I went to the dance dressed in my preppy best: a dark blue winter sport coat, khaki pants with the buckled tab on the back, a pale blue shirt with a button-down collar, striped tie and white buck shoes.   The dance was a low-keyd affair with very few guys in attendance.   Fay seemed happy to see me, if a little surprised. She danced well and we got along, though she was much more reserved than I remembered. That surprised me after the attention she showered on me the first time we met. *There is ice to be melted here before I can win her over*, I thought.

When Fay learned that I had dropped out of college, she seemed disappointed and even more reserved. She questioned why I did such a thing. She showed concern about my future prospects, and hers with me. I tried to make a date with her, but she did not commit. She didn't seem to want to foster a relationship with me. I, however, was becoming even more fascinated with her. The next time I called her for a date she again tried to discourage me. What I didn't know was how interested she was in a jock from John Carroll, a local university.

Maybe I should look elsewhere, I wondered. Thoughts of that cute little blonde, Judy again popped into my head. *Nah, she lived too far away*. Back to Fay, but first a little research. *She intrigued me, but why?* I still didn't know, so I asked DJ. He had no idea.

To find out more information, I went back to my old standby of asking questions. I called Fay and asked her a few. "What are you majoring in at college?"

"History," she answered and went silent.

"I love history. What period?"

"American History," she said. I carried on a conversation with her about American History. Before my next call, I pulled out my high school history book and studied it. She was fascinated by my grasp of the subject. I stayed a chapter ahead of her in our later conversations. She never did seem to catch on to my game.

Out of the blue, my sister, Betty Malesardi, called from New Jersey. It was very unusual to get a long distance telephone call in those days. They were very expensive. "Bob [her husband] will be passing through Cleveland and has a layover at the city airport," she said. "Will you go out and meet him? I'd like you to get to know each other better." Betty lived in New York City when she met Bob. The only time I met him was at their wedding. Now she was hoping I'd make an effort to see him.

"Yes," I promised. The airport was on Fay's side of town, so I asked her to join me.

"Pick me up at work and I'll join you," she said. She clerked at *Saks Fifth Avenue,* a fancy women's apparel shop close to the airport. "You can take me home afterward. It'll save my family the trouble of making the trip," she said without much sensitivity.

Fay was dressed in a dark blue suit with a short skirt, an elegant and stylish outfit. The jacket pulled across the bust, accentuating it. Her short skirt revealed shapely legs, especially when she sat down. The nylons with black high-heeled shoes gave her a sophisticated look. I was mighty proud to be walking through the airport with her. The place was filled with well-dressed people.

This was my first time at such a large airport. I didn't feel confident about knowing my way around. I had to be careful not to look inexperienced while trying to impress Fay. Upon checking at the ticket counter we learned that Bob's flight wasn't due for another half-hour.

"Let's go to the coffee shop for a drink," I suggested. As we sat down at a table, I noticed a sharp looking airline hostess sitting at the counter with two guys. I took them to be airline pilots by their uniforms. The hostess took one look in our direction and shot off her stool. She tapped one of the pilots on the shoulder and said something to him. With a flick of her head, she indicated that he take a look in our direction. He did and stopped to stare. I turned to see who they were watching, expecting to see somebody famous behind me. There was nobody behind me. Then the pilot grabbed his fellow pilot by the arm. They both looked our way. Fay was obviously the center of their attention.   Well, why not? Fay was sharp, well-built and looked chic.   Fay was sitting across the table from me and hadn't noticed the trio.   She was unaware of their attention.   She talked to me while I took in the show.   They apparently thought she was some celebrity.

My brother-in-law, Bob Malesardi, was sitting near his airline gate when we returned.   He was wearing a bright red jacket, gold tie and a blue shirt with a button-down collar.   When he stood up to greet us his trousers screamed out, "Here I am." They were bright Madras plaid in colors matching his tie, jacket, shirt and every other color in the rainbow.   Bob was a high-powered businessman and always a flashy dresser.   I complimented him on his outfit, though I thought it truly bizarre.

"I just bought it in California," Bob said.   "Most fashion trends start out there and then move to New York," he instructed us.   "I like being ahead of my fellow New Yorkers."

"I work at *Saks Fifth Avenue*," Fay said.   "I appreciate your fashion sense."

"Thank you," Bob replied, "I know that chain of stores.   Why don't we go to the bar for a drink?" he suggested.   We all ordered soft drinks.   Once we got comfortable, Bob said, "By the way, Fay, has anyone ever told you that you look just like Audrey Hepburn the movie star?" Fay beamed.   She couldn't have been more pleased.

Then it dawned on me: the pilots back at the coffee shop probably thought Fay was Audrey Hepburn.   In my car on our way to Fay's home, I told her about the scene with the pilots.   She was pleased to hear the story.

"Why didn't you tell me about it at the time?" she asked.

"I didn't know what was going on then.

"You don't know who Audrey Hepburn is?" she asked in amazement.

"No. Sorry. I don't get to many movies."

"She's starring in a new movie called *Sabrina* this weekend at *The Palace* downtown." That was one of those movie castles in the downtown area of Cleveland. "I think you'll love her."

"Why don't I take you to see the movie?" I suggested. She finally agreed to a date. Apparently, Fay wanted me to see the movie so I would appreciate just how much she looked like the star. That was fine with me. Now at least I had a date with her.

On the way back to the east side after dropping Fay at her home, I got one of my more audacious ideas. I decided to pull a joke on her. I called the *Cleveland Plain Dealer,* our local newspaper, and I told them, "Audrey Hepburn will be in town for a sneak preview of her new movie opening downtown. If you promise to wait until after the movie, I will tell you which showing she'll be attending. You can take all the pictures you want of her as she comes out of the theater, but not before." They promised to cooperate and never even asked who I was.

Fay was excited about going to see the new movie starring Audrey Hepburn. I picked her up at her home on Lake Avenue on the west side and drove downtown to *The Palace Theatre*.

The movie *Sabrina* starred William Holden and Humphrey Bogart, two of my favorites. Fay loved the movie and I could certainly see the resemblance between Audrey Hepburn and Fay. In fact, it was obvious Fay was going out of her way to look like Audrey Hepburn. Fay had the same short bobbed haircut, heavy dark eyebrows, and dark red lipstick. Miss Hepburn was adorable, as was Fay! Miss Hepburn was slim and elfin while Fay had a much better build.

This was the first time I had seen Hepburn in a movie. Where had I been? Well, I was out of the country most of 1953, and part of 1954 while I was in the Navy, then to college where we didn't go to the movies.

It was impressive to view the movie in one of those old-time palatial theaters. As we strolled into the grand lobby afterward we discussed it excitedly. Even I had forgotten about the press. Flash bulbs started popping before I realized what was happening. A reporter rushed us, totally ignoring me as he questioned Fay. She couldn't grasp what was happening. She thought he was just trying to get her impressions of the movie as a theatergoer. She gave it a glowing report. Then she realized he was calling her, "Miss Hepburn."

By this time, people, some asking for autographs, had surrounded us. I took charge and led Fay through the crowd pushing people out of the way when necessary, but I didn't say a word. As we cleared the front doors of the theater, a taxicab was unloading a couple. I commandeered the taxicab and literally pushed Fay into the back seat before I slammed the door closed. I ran around to the other side and hopped in as I told the driver, "Take off!" He roared off as the crowd rushed curbside. After swinging into traffic he chanced a look into his rearview mirror. By the look on his face I could tell he, too, thought Fay was Miss Hepburn. The pride on his face showed this.

"Where to?" the driver asked. I directed him to my car. On seeing my '50 Chevy, he became somewhat confused.

"Is that your car?" he asked. I tipped him without an explanation.

"Well, that was exciting!" I said as I got into the car. Fay hadn't said a word. Apparently she didn't know what to think of it.

Finally she said, without looking at me. "Did you have anything to do with that fiasco?"

"Me, how would I be able to pull that off?" I said with a straight face. She didn't know me very well, yet! In fact, she had referred to me as a callow youth on more than one occasion. She had no idea how old I was. In fact, she didn't know that I had already served in the Navy during the Korean War before going to college. She just thought I was a freshman in college.

At Fay's request, we started to hang around a bar called *The Cottage Inn*, a hangout for the John Carroll college crowd. Fay liked the place. I still didn't realize she was looking for her jock friend. I recognized a lot of the people there from my summertime stays at Geneva and Madison-on-the-Lake. Word spread that there was going to be a big college party the following Saturday night.

"Can you get us an invitation?" Fay asked me. She desperately wanted to go. I got the invitation.

"Can you get a date for my cousin, Sue?" Sue had been DJ's date over Christmas when the six of us went dancing.

"How about Frank Joyce," I kidded her. She gave me a dirty look. Frank had not been a pleasant date for Fay that night.

About that time Sam, a friend of mine, walked up to us. I signaled to Fay indicating, "What about him?" Fay nodded in approval. "How would you like a date for Saturday night?" I asked Sam. "We're going to a party and Fay has a nice looking cousin I can fix you up with."

Sam took one look at Fay and said, "Sure." He must have assumed Sue would be as pretty as Fay.

Saturday night, I picked up Sam and we took the long drive to the west side of town using the Edgewater Parkway. That road ran alongside Lake Erie. I was happy to have Sam for company.

We picked up the girls. I could tell Sam liked his date by the look on his face. To my surprise, both girls got into the back seat. *Sue must be more shy than I thought.* We no sooner got back on the Parkway when a terrible rainstorm hit. I could hardly see where I was going. The Parkway was a divided highway with two lanes going east and west. Cars were stopping right in the middle of the highway. "This is too dangerous," I announced to the gang. "I'm getting off this highway before we ram somebody in their back end," I said, as I pulled off at the Metro Parkway exit. The Edgewater, a raised highway, ran over the Metro. I didn't think about it at the time as we spiraled down the exit. Pulling onto the Metro we ran into a river of water that was supposed to be the road. I continued as I knew the Metro rose a few hundred feet ahead. We didn't make it! The water continued to rise until it flooded our engine, stopping the car and killing all power including the headlights. The water kept rising and actually came inside the passenger's compartment.

"We're going to drown!" the girls screamed. They discussed their imminent deaths while I pondered our situation. We had to pull our legs up onto the seats to keep them out of the water. Fortunately, the water stopped just below the top of our seats.

"Now what are we going to do?" Sam asked just before the girls asked the same thing.

"We're stuck here for a while," I observed.

"What'll my parents say when we don't come home tonight?" Sue asked.

"What're we going to do now?" Sam asked again.

"I don't know about you, but I plan to have a drink," I said. "Fay, please pass me the bag from the back shelf." The bag contained the supplies for the party. It had a bag of ice, a bottle of scotch, some paper cups, and a bottle of club soda in it. "Anyone for a drink," I asked.

It wasn't long before the four of us were feeling no pain. The girls giggled as I told stories of some of my more harrowing experiences with flood waters and cars. Fortunately, the water finally started to recede.

"Now that the water has gone down, maybe I can get the engine started," I said. "To do this I'll have to get under the hood of the car." My plan was to dry the ignition wires. Taking off my suit coat and tie I handed them to Fay to put on the back shelf. Then I removed my shoes and socks. After rolling up my pants' legs as high as they would go, I opened the car door and stepped out. Putting all my mechanical car skills to work, I dried the ignition system's wires. I climbed back into the car. Sure enough, the engine started when I turned the key. Slowly, I moved the car ahead to the cheers of my companions. Out of the river onto higher ground we went. I was the hero of the hour. As I continued up the hill, the girls realized I wasn't taking them home.

"Where do you think you're going now?" Fay asked.

"We're going to the party!" I proclaimed.

We passed through many deeply flooded roads before getting to the party house. Only this time, I checked the situation before venturing into any flood water. Each time the girls, now experts on engine problems, protested saying, "You're going to flood the engine again." I never entered a flooded area until I saw another car make it through without a problem. When we reached the party house, it was dark. In fact, the whole neighborhood had lost their electricity.

"Where to now," Sam asked.

"Take us home," the girls demanded.

"It's early yet, besides, I don't want to get back on that highway until the water has a chance to go down." We went to the *Cottage Inn*. The bar had lights and cold beer. The place was hopping. All our party friends were there. I wandered through the crowd, telling the story of our harrowing experience. The tale grew with each telling. "Mr. Jock" happened upon Fay sitting at a table with Sue and Sam.

"Who're you with?" he asked her.

"Mark Kelly; do you know him?" She turned to introduce me. I was not there!

"No. Do you?" he quipped. Ignoring his wisecrack, Fay turned and spied me across the room talking to some friends. I looked a mess! Though my suit coat was back on, my pants and shirt looked like they had been dipped into the river, wrung out and put back on without bothering to dry them. She decided not to introduce me to "Mr. Jock" that evening.

Moving

The University of Dayton informed me that I could return for the fall semester. When it became time to go back to UD, Frank Joyce, Dick Heil, Pat Dowling and I traveled to Dayton to find a place to live. One of my former roommates, Ivan Stemley, who lived in Dayton, invited us to stay with him until we found a place.

Pat hung up the telephone. "I've got great news. I found a place for us to live. It's right across the street from the school library." *Talk about a great location. That solves my number one rule: live close to the campus,* I thought.

"Thank you Mrs. Stemley for the great breakfast," Pat said. "Ham and eggs never tasted so good. And thank you for letting us stay here until we found a place of our own."

"Don't be in such a hurry to move out," she said. "I plan to feed you another great meal tonight. We enjoy your company. Don't we Gene?"

"Sure stay as long as you like," Gene Stemley said. We called him Ivan, his middle name. It described his unique personality more than Gene did. He taught me how to meet girls and keep them entertained.

"I also want to thank you for the potato salad and hamburgers last night," Dick Heil said. He was another of my former roommates from *The Mansion.* We were planning to be roommates again for the upcoming semester at the university.

"Boy, I can't believe you found a place right across the street from UD," I remarked to Pat as we headed for our cars. "Tell us more about it."

"It's a two-story duplex," Pat explained. "Mark, why don't you follow us in your car? The place is located at 4213 Alberta Street. We have our own parking behind the duplex. Meet us there."

As we parked and got out of our cars I remarked, "Boy, is this great! There're four parking places."

"Two of them belong to the guys in the other half of the duplex," Pat said. "But before we go in I better warn you. There's one slight problem."

"What's that?" I asked.

"It's unfurnished."

"Are you nuts? Where're we going to get furniture?" I roared.

"We'll work on that later. That's why the place is still available and so cheap."

"How cheap?" I asked.

"It cost $50 a month, plus utilities." I realized that Dick was being surprisingly quiet all this time.   Well, he's always up for a challenge. "By the way, I already said we'd take the place," Pat said. "You can change your mind if you don't like it."

We walked in the back door, which I noticed was unlocked. It led straight into the kitchen.   "Well, it does have a stove," Dick remarked.

I opened one of the cabinets, "But no dishes."

"We can bring them from home along with any pots and pans our parents are willing to give us," Pat suggested.

"Look at the nice finish on the woodwork and stairs," Dick remarked.   It was then that I remembered his father was in the moving business.   Dick noticed things like that.

"It's mahogany," Pat said proudly.

As we passed the stairs, which went both up to the second floor and down to the basement I said, "There's not a stick of furniture in here."

"But look at the great mahogany mantle and fireplace in the front room," Dick again pointed out.   "And the floors are freshly finished mahogany also."

"I wonder what the upstairs looks like," Pat said.   "I understand there are three bedrooms."

"I hope there's a bathroom," I said sarcastically.

"Look, all the woodwork is newly finished," Dick pointed out proudly.   Upstairs Dick walked directly down the hall to the front bedroom.   "I claim this room for Frank Joyce and me," he said.

"It's plenty big enough for the two of us."

"Mark, why don't you and I take this second bedroom," Pat said. "It's small, but we should fit in it all right." I was proud Pat picked me as his roommate. After all, he was a mover and shaker on campus as well as a senior.

"This bathroom is fine," Dick said.

"But there is no shower," I pointed out.

"Who needs a shower?" Dick said.

"Look, here is the third bedroom," Pat said.

"It's not much bigger than the bathroom," I pointed out. "It won't hold more than one guy."

"Let's check the basement," Pat suggested. Down we went again admiring the woodwork.

"There's only one light down here and it's a naked bulb hanging from a wire," Dick observed.

"Yeah, but there's a washing machine," Pat pointed out.

"Boy, that old time wringer thing?" I blurted. "I don't think we'll be using it."

"Mark, you're spoiled. I remember how you loved the laundry facilities back at *The Mansion,*" Dick said.

"You know what?" I declared. "I can rig a shower down here in the basement over that floor drain." I remembered how my dad always built a bathroom in the basement. "All we need is a garden hose and a shower head," I said getting into the swing of things. "I have tools in my car. And I can go to the hardware store and get all the things I need."

"Mark, why don't you do that," Pat said. "By the way, there's the furnace and it looks fairly new."

"Dick, why don't you come with me," Pat said. "I hear that they're getting rid of some bunk beds at St. John's." And off they went. *Wherever that is,* I thought.

I went to the hardware store while Dick and Pat went scouting. I was plumbing the shower when the guys burst into the house shouting and carrying on. I ran up the stairs. "What the heck is going on?" I asked.

"We have four bunk beds. We bought them from St. John's. It's a seminary owned by UD. We'll assemble them while you finish the shower."

Later Dick said, "We're going out to see what else we can find," and off they went. They returned with some plywood scaffolding they had pilfered from a construction site.

"What on earth are you going to do with that stuff?" I asked in horror. "It's covered with concrete droppings and dust."

"Build a bar. We can put it right here," Dick said pointing at the wall in the dining room next to the stairs going up.

"Good luck," I said. "You'll never get that stuff off the wood. It won't be clean enough to make a bar out of it."

Much to my surprise, the finished product was magnificent! The top of the bar became a highly polished stained surface any bar owner would be proud to have in his establishment. The face of the bar was decorated with nude dancing girls painted by one of Dick's more beautiful and talented art student girlfriends.

"Look what I found," Dick said proudly. He had a stuffed deer head with a large rack of antlers slung over his shoulder. My roommates made many scavenger hunts through the neighborhood alleys picking through the trash.   They even acquired a kitchen table and chairs.

"What are you going to do with that thing?" I asked pointing to the deer head.

"Hang it over our rather fine fireplace in the front room," he said. We named him *Rudolf*, the deer, of course. Anyone passing by could easily spot *Rudolf through* the front window since we didn't have any curtains. The deer sported a bright red nose, a tie with our school colors – blue and red—sunglasses and a cigarette sticking out of its mouth. The only other piece of paraphernalia sitting on the mantle looked like a three-inch tall silver whistle. It stuck out like an igloo on Maui. Why it was there was anybody's guess and no one was saying.

The gang promised to return to school with whatever their parents let them take. This included a full set of dishes, pots and pans, an assortment of lamps and a few small tables for our bedrooms.

"Let's throw a party," Dick suggested.   In spite of the lack of furniture, it was decided we'd do just that.   "I'll plan the decorations," Dick volunteered. "We have to find some of those wine bottles wrapped with straw," he insisted.

"Why?" I asked.

"To put on each table," Dick answered.

"What tables? We only have the one in the kitchen."

"We'll borrow more," he said with a wave of the hand. Sure enough, we borrowed three tables. Dick found some of his wine bottles wrapped in straw in a trash container behind a fancy bar. "We have to cover the bottles with dripped wax," Dick insisted.

"What are the bottles for," I asked.

"We'll put candles in them and use them for the party lights. They'll be the only lights we'll use," he explained. "They'll create ambiance for our party. And we're going to cover the floors with straw to give the place atmosphere."

"Are you crazy?" I blurted. "Card tables are not very stable. If one of those candles falls to the floor, this place will go up in flames before you can shout, *Fire*." He wouldn't listen to reason and the other guys acquiesced. Dick spent hours dripping wax on those bottles.

The night of the party we had three card tables set up in the living and dining rooms. The only light we had was furnished by a single candle on each table. And yes, there was straw covering the floors everywhere. Our washing machine contained a large amount of orange juice.

Dick greeted each new couple at the door, "Did you bring your entrance fee?" To questioning looks he explained, "Your entrance fee is a bottle of booze. When they showed him their bottle, he said, "We want you to pour it into this washing machine."

"In there?" came their questioning response.

"Yup, in there. We're making a giant cocktail." After each bottle was poured, Dick would hit the switch causing the machine to oscillate, mixing the drink. The guys usually smiled in delight. Their dates looked horrified. "Now let's test the cocktail to see how it tastes," Dick encouraged.

The girls still wouldn't drink our delectable concoction. But the lights were low, the candles the only source of light, the mood romantic. The party rocked on to the music supplied by our record player and no one set the place ablaze. From that night on, our place became known as *The Dirty Double*.

Anytime someone asked me where I lived I would say, "*The Dirty Double*."

Their usual response was, "Yeah, I know where that is." Even girls I met responded with recognition. It wasn't the name we chose, but the name given to it by many of the student body who thought they knew the place well.

There were two different versions to the story about why our home at college was called *The Dirty Double* depending on which student was telling the story. Some said it was because of the raucous parties thrown there on a regular basis by the rather loose bunch of individuals living there. The other version of the story was that the place was filthy because the guys living there never cleaned up after their first party.

The Dirty Double

Ivan Stemley decided to move in with us even though he had to sleep on the couch. As school got underway, all our housemates went to each Saturday afternoon football game except Pat. He would just disappear. I figured he didn't like football.

One day I asked Dick, "What's the significance of that mouthpiece sitting on the mantle?" I expected one of his truly bizarre answers.

It belongs to Pat," Dick explained. "He's in the school's marching band. That's why he never comes to any of the games with us. He is marching on the field."

"I guess I don't know my roommate very well."

When my brother John heard me mentioning Pat Dowling's name he said, "I know him. He was a State Wrestling Champ in high school." *So much for knowing my roommate*, I thought.

Cincinnati Enquirer

On a warm, early fall afternoon as I strolled home, I met Kevin O'Neill coming up the hill. "Did you read the Cincinnati

Enquirer today?" he asked me.

"I don't even read the Dayton papers. Why would I read one from Cincinnati?"

"There's a story on the front page, I think you'll find it fascinating," he said. "It's about a college prank at the University of Cincinnati. Somebody painted the statues, Mic and Mac, the lions that are supposed to be guarding the school. They painted them blue and red. UD's school colors," he explained.

"Why should this concern me?"

"The Cincinnati Enquirer is insinuating the vandals were from the University of Dayton. They're urging the students to retaliate. They just about said that students should come up here and paint our lions with U of C colors."

"Well, they're our archrivals, after all. We play them in football and basketball every year. Some of our students probably did go to their school and paint the lions," I suggested.

"That's right! You guys in the *Dirty Double* should stand guard tonight. After all, you live right across the street from the library where they're sure to strike," Kevin pointed out.

"Not a bad idea," I agreed. "I'll suggest it to Dick Heil. It's just the kind of thing to get him worked up."

"Dick," I said, as I entered the house. "Did you hear what happened at the University of Cincinnati last night?"

"No, and who cares?"

"You will," I explained. "The Cincinnati Enquirer is telling the whole city that some of the University of Dayton students painted the U of C lions using our school colors. The Enquirer wants the student body to retaliate. Don't you think we should stand guard tonight? Our library is the natural target."

"You're right," he said.   By the look on his face, I could tell his mind had kicked into gear.   "We'll have to light up the place so they can't get near it without us spotting them.   Wait.   I got a better idea.   Let's put lights in the trees and have the on/off switch here in our house.   We can stun them when they think they're in total darkness and about to do the dirty deed."

"How are we going to do that?" I asked.

"I know a guy in the school photo lab," Pat Dowling said. He had been listening to our conversation.

"I didn't know we had a photo lab," I said.

"I'll borrow some floodlights from him," Pat said.   "We can mount them in the trees on the library lawn,"

"How are you going to wire them up?" I asked, ever the engineer.

"We'll run an extension cord from our house to the lights," Dick chimed in, agreeing with the plan.

"You'll blow a fuse.   We'll lose all the power in our house including those flood lights," I pointed out.   "They'll escape in the dark."

"Kelly, you're the engineer.   You figure out how to keep that from happening.   We'll figure out how to mount the lights," Pat recommended.   I grudgingly thought *He's giving me a lot of credit for electrical knowledge, along with a big job*.   I used my knowledge learned in the Navy to check out our electrical system in *The Dirty Double*.   At the fuse box, I picked out the circuit with the least appliances as our best source of electricity for the floodlights.   In fact, other than the refrigerator, we had very few electrical appliances on any of our circuits.

"Yep, this should work," I said to Frank Joyce, who didn't seem a bit interested. He just sat there sipped on his beer. If he had any interest in our household project, it certainly wasn't enough to help. "But just in case, I'll go to the hardware store and buy a stronger fuse that'll increase our capacity," I concluded.

Dick walked into the house just after I had replaced the fuses. "We've got the floodlights up in the trees," He said. "Mark, are you ready for the big test?

"Plug the extension cord into this outlet," I said, pointing at the one under the front window.

"Are they on?" Dick yelled to Pat, who was standing in the middle of the library lawn. "Pat is waving his arms in the air," Dick shouted. "That's the signal they're working."

"Let's leave them on for a few minutes to be sure they don't blow the fuse," I suggested. "Perfect, the lights work, and the fuse didn't blow," I said after a while. "Let's pull the plug now."

"We're going to need some help handling these culprits," Dick pointed out. "We don't know how many guys will show up from their school."

"I'll get a couple of my buddies to man the pay telephone on the top floor of Alumni Hall," Pat said. "They can have guys on each floor ready to alert the entire dorm when we need their help. We can make one telephone call and they can spread the word."

"I had no problem recruiting students," Pat explained when he returned to *The Dirty Double*," I hyped the story so well about protecting our school that probably half the guys from the dorm are willing to help us."

"I stopped to talk to our one and only campus guard to tell him about the plan," said John Saggio, one of our better-connected roommates. "The guard is scared stiff they'll beat him to a pulp before we get there to help him. I told the guard not to worry. I recruited three football players to ride with him tonight."

Being autumn, it got dark early. We had all the lights on in the house. "We better keep all the lights off in our house tonight to improve our night vision," I explained to the group. "I learned that in the Navy."

"You were in the Navy?" somebody said in surprise. So I told them stories about my naval experience to pass the time while we waited. "One of us should wait on the front porch where he'll have a better view," I suggested. "We'll take turns standing guard so we don't go to sleep out there."

"Fat chance any of us will fall asleep tonight." Pat pointed out.

"There they are," Dick whispered. "Pat, call the dorm. Mark, get ready to turn on the flood lights at my command." Pat made the call. "We'll wait until the intruders are just about to mount the steps of the library."

"Throw the switch," Dick yelled at the top of his lungs.

The incredible burst of lights stopped the predators in their tracks. "Charge!" yelled Dick as the five of us burst across the street. We surrounded the six of them.

"How do you puny little guys think you're going to stop us?" asked one of the big intruders. He had a good point. They all looked like giant football players and we weren't in very good shape. As they contemplated beating us to a pulp, a massive herd of students came rushing over the hill next to the library screaming their lungs out.

"My God, it's the entire student body!" yelled one of their guys as our students surrounded them.

"Take them to *The Dirty Double*," yelled Dick at the top of his lungs. "Follow me." The crowd had no problem handling the intruders.

Once we got inside *The Dirty Double*, Saggio said, "There must be over a hundred guys standing on our porch and in our front yard."

"And we're packed in here," Pat needlessly pointed out. "Guys are still coming in the back door. The kitchen is full too."

"What are we going to do with these U of C students?" somebody asked.

"Shave their heads," I shouted, remembering how humiliating that was when it happened to me in the Navy. "First cut their hair with these scissors while I get my electric razor."

"Sit them on these kitchen chairs," Dick said. "I volunteer to be the barber."

"Dick, leave enough hair so I can shave the letter "D" for Dayton on the top of his head. That way, his whole university will know what happened to him when he tried to defile our school."

"Father Collins, the Dean of Students, is coming," the word passed through the crowd. "He looks like Moses parting the Red Sea. Guys are disappearing as he comes."

"I'm getting out of here," the gang said as they rushed for the back door. I had already shaved "Ds" in two heads when Father Collins walked in. Those that couldn't get out of the house because they were jammed in the room went dead silent.

Father surveyed the room. We figured we'd all be expelled from college that very night. "I don't see anything wrong here," he said. He turned and walked out the front door. Some say he had a smile on his face.

"We better quit while we're ahead," Pat said. "No pun intended. Let these guys go and everyone get back to their dorm before Father comes back."

Two days later, Pat announced waving a newspaper over his head, "Did you see the story in the Cincinnati Enquirer? They're asking, what is this new trend in college, where guys are shaving the letter "D" on the tops of their heads."

15.
Cup of Tea
Celia P. Ransom

Today I had a cup of tea.
My lost friend's face flashed in front of me.
Tea was what we always shared
'cause for coffee she never cared.
And there I sat with hands on cup
Remembering subjects we might have brought up.
Mostly t'would be the foibles of family
But perhaps the world's state, its lack of morality.
Or—at this time of year
It might be the holidays, Christmas being near.
And there I sat without her at my side
The sting of loss, almost more than I could abide.
Looking into my empty cup
Remembering a life to god given up.

16.
Disasters
Mark A. Kelly

Where To Live?

College did not start well for me. The class work was easy enough, but my living conditions were not. Jim Holecek, my high school buddy and I, did not think that college dorm life would suit us, twenty-one -year-old war Veterans. We would be subjected to a nightly curfew and not be able to drink in our rooms. We elected to rent a room across the street from the campus.

That proved to have its drawbacks. The landlady did not look kindly on us coming and going at all hours of the night. Bringing booze and girls into the house was out of the question. Not that Jim was interested in any girls other than his one true love, Pat Corsaro, his girlfriend back in Cleveland. Jim and I had limited kitchen privileges at the rooming house and had to eat our meals out. The school cafeteria food did not appeal to us, but eating out was expensive. It was time to find more accommodating living arrangements.

Jim got an offer to move into a house with two guys, El Carlini, and Tony DiSanto, from his old neighborhood in Cleveland. I was apprehensive about the fact that they were members of a neighborhood gang called the *Bone Crushers*. One summer at the cottage at Madison-on-the-Lake, Ohio, during high school, some of my friends, Bill Kennedy, Art Holan and I, had a run in with that gang. The *Bone Crushers* tried to push us around. Bill saw the need to crush a few bones himself, as he broke the jaw of one of them. Art and Bill were star football players and nobody to mess with. I was not sure if El or Tony would remember me since that happened more than three years ago.

El invited Jim and me to take a look at his digs. "I'll pick you up at your rooming house at four o'clock this afternoon and drive you to my place," El said. Fortunately, neither he nor Tony remembered me from that summer at the cottage. El drove through downtown Dayton and across the river north to Salem Avenue.

"Whoa, where'r we going?" I asked.

"It's just a few more blocks," he said. "Look at these homes. They look like mansions," he pointed out to us. "Here we are." El pulled into the driveway behind one of the mansions. "This is it. We live in what used to be the carriage house belonging to this mansion. They converted it into two townhouses. Now we're living in the lap of luxury." He parked his car at the end of a long two story carriage house.

"Where is it?" I asked.

"It's the second townhouse straight ahead," El said. "Two young girls live in this first one." As we walked past their unit, I studied the surroundings. The mansion was in good shape with a large back yard. The townhouses sat on the opposite end of the property. I was impressed. El opened the door to his place and stepped aside, giving us a full view of the living room. Dark red wall-to-wall carpeting covered the large living room floor. Light from the front window reflected off the stucco plaster walls. There was a couch along one wall with tables and lamps at either end. A low coffee table sat in front of it. There was plenty of room for the two additional upholstered chairs. The high ceilings made the place look like a palatial Hollywood movie set.

"Here is a bathroom," El said opening a door just off the living room. It was better than any bathroom the Kelly's ever had.

"The kitchen is straight ahead." The tile floor reflected the light from the window on the opposite wall. I liked the fact that the house was bright inside. Not dark like our rooming house.

"You can see there is plenty of room for the breakfast table and four chairs. Look at all the cabinets above and below the counter. We have a complete set of dishes, pots and pans. The refrigerator is brand new." El allowed us plenty of time to take in the place.

"Would you like to take a look at the upstairs?" El invited. He turned into the hall at the bottom of the stairs. The dark red carpeted steps led up to a landing also lit by the window at the top of the stairs. The first door off the upstairs hallway opened into a spacious bedroom with a twin bed along each wall. There was a large closet. The door at the end of the hall opened into another large bedroom with a spacious closet. The upstairs bath was large and well equipped. The place was a palace compared to our current living quarters.

"We have full use of multiple washers and dryers located in the basement of the mansion," El added. "And they are free."

"Let's go for a drink while we discuss the other advantages of living here," El suggested. He took us to a bar on Salem Avenue called *Sully's,* just a few blocks away. From the outside, the place looked like a common neighborhood bar. As we stepped inside my mood changed instantly. A lush red leather bench ran the entire length of the south wall. Tables and chairs were spaced in front of the long bench. The minute I took my seat, I felt like I had joined a friendly private party. A group of twelve guys were sitting together just a couple of tables away. They were enjoying pitchers of beer spaced among them as they laughed and joked.

"They come here every Tuesday evening just to entertain themselves," El explained. "Wait until you hear them sing." El ordered and paid for a pitcher of beer for us. At that, the group began to harmonize. They sang college drinking songs better than any fraternity I'd ever heard.

We sat drinking our beer, too entranced to interrupt the music. Then a thought entered my head, *we are being diverted from our task at hand. Do Jim and I really want to live this far from the campus?* When the group took a break, I said to El, "It's unfortunate that your place is located on the north side of town while UD's campus is on the south side."

"I'll drive you to and from school," El promised. "As you can see, I have a brand new 1954 Ford convertible.

"I'll have to think it over," I told El. Jim nodded in agreement. We didn't do much thinking that evening. When we got back to our rooming house, we practically passed out from all the free beer El bought for us.

"What do you think?" I asked Jim the next night as we ate our usual meal at a local restaurant.

"Boy wasn't that a great time last night?" he responded.

"Best I've had since coming to college," I admitted. "But let's weigh the pros and cons of changing our living arrangements."

"The distance between the two places favors the rooming house," Jim pointed out.

"If you add the cost of our room and eating out and compare it to the cost projected by El, we can afford to live there including a weekly stop at *Sully's,*" I said. That did it! We decided to move in with El and Tony and share expenses. That included helping with the cooking. To mentally justify the long drive to school, we started to refer to our new digs as *The Mansion*.

To get to school in time for the eight o'clock class, our routine began early. El was only going to make one trip. That meant we all left together whether we had a morning class or not. We ate breakfast, and then the four of us El, Tony, Jim and I piled into El's car for the ride to campus. We met at the Student Union about four in the afternoon for the ride home.

Most of my classes were in the morning. This meant that I had to kill time waiting for El to drive us back to the *Mansion*. I was getting mighty tired of all this waiting. Worse yet, I had an evening class two nights a week. Professor Oskar Hauenstein's engineering drawing class killed my ride home. El and the gang were long gone by the time I got out of class at ten o'clock. If the bus did not come immediately, I started to walk. Many nights I could not run fast enough to catch the bus at the next stop. The buses ran so infrequently at that hour I usually ended up walking all the way across town, a trip of three miles. I did not mind, I loved *The Mansion* and was very proud to tell people where I lived.

It was at this time I started to learn some new life lessons. The first lesson was—the next time I am looking for new college lodgings; make sure it is close to the campus.

Homecoming

My roommate, Jim and I sat in *The Mansion* one Thursday night contemplating the lonely upcoming weekend. We were feeling sorry for ourselves. We had left our girlfriends behind in Cleveland and gone off to college. Hitchhiking home took as long as eight hours one way and now, with winter coming, we had decided to stay in Dayton this weekend.

"Why don't we invite the girls to the Homecoming Dance?" Jim suggested.

"Great idea," I agreed. "I'll see if Marilynn is busy." She was thrilled at the prospect of going to a college dance. Marilynn is coming," I told Jim. "I'll call Pat to see what she thinks of the idea." We both knew Pat was dying for an invitation to Dayton. "The plans are set," Jim informed me. "I'll call Pat to see what she thinks of the idea." We both knew Pat was dying for an invitation to Dayton. "The plans are set," Jim informed me.

El, one of our other roommates, overheard us discussing plans for the dance. "You can use my car," El offered. "I won't need it. I'm double-dating with a buddy." This was an enormous favor. El had a brand new 1954 Ford Crestline Sunliner Convertible, the glamour queen of cars.

The dance was held in a huge ballroom at Lakeside Amusement Park in northwest Dayton. We joined the long line at the entrance. While standing there, I relished the thought of dancing with my sweetie, holding her close in my arms. We were at the door of the dance hall before we realized it. The gatekeeper stopped us.

"Let see what's in your purses," he demanded of the girls. After checking, he waved them in. "What's in the paper bag?" he asked me. The girls looked back in horror as he pulled out a bottle of Seagram's gin followed by a bottle of Seven Crown whiskey.

"Okay, go on in."

"What was he looking for?" Marilynn asked in amazement." She did not know that we were allowed to bring alcohol into the dancehall.

"Pop or mix for our drinks. They don't allow you to bring them into the dancehall," I explained to her. "You have to buy theirs. That's how they make their money. The dancehall does not have a liquor license."

Thank God, El told us about this ahead of time. This was our first college dance and we knew nothing about the routine.

The inside of the dancehall reminded me of *The Pier*, at Geneva-on-the-Lake; where I worked as a ticket-taker at the tender age of ten the early 1940s. It looked like a huge wooden barn, dimly lit with tables wrapped around the dance floor. In contrast, the bandstand looked like it was lit by the sun. The light sparkled off the music stands and drum set. An eight-piece orchestra dressed in dark formal attire played swing music reminiscent of the 1940s. Even the music reminded me of *The Pier.*

Every table was full or had people holding seats for their friends. Even our roommates' table was full. We had to go to the back corner of the hall to find a table. Jim and Pat did not mind as they wanted to be alone. Marilynn and I gave them their space by dancing the night away. We both loved to dance and I liked the feel of Marilynn's warm body next to mine as we danced to the slow numbers like *Your Cheatin Heart* and *Stranger in Paradise.* While catching our breath after fast dancing to the song *Shake Rattle and Roll,* Marilynn spotted Jim Synk, a friend of hers from Cleveland.

"What are you doing here?" he asked in surprise. Apparently they were good friends.

"I'm with Mark Kelly," she answered introducing me. "Mark was a classmate of yours in high school," Marilynn told Jim.

"I'm sorry I don't remember you," he said with no sorrow in his voice. Though I knew him, I was not surprised he did not know me. There were over three-hundred-fifty guys in our graduating class. Here at UD, he was already a junior having gone directly to college after high school. I had gone into the Navy before college and now I was only a freshman.

After the big dance, Jim and Pat could not bear to part. Though it was almost one in the morning, I suggested the four of us go out for breakfast. That gave them more time to be together.

We found an all-night diner close to *The Mansion*. While we were eating, the waitress raced over to our table.

"Are you driving a green Ford Convertible?" she asked frantically.

"Yes. Why?" I asked.

"Some guy just hit your car and he is taking off," she yelled.

"Call the police!" I screamed in panic as I raced out of the restaurant. Sure enough, the guy had sideswiped El's car while attempting to park. Now he was trying to leave before getting caught.

"You hit my car!" I screamed banging on the driver's side window. He almost knocked me over as he swung out of his parking spot. We had parked on a diagonal in the single line of parking spaces behind the diner. To get out of the lot he now had to drive forward. In desperation, I stood in front of his car blocking the way. This confused him long enough for the police to arrive.

"This guy sideswiped my car and is trying to get away," I told the cop. For the first time, I got a good look at the crease along El's car door. *He is going to kill me!* I thought.

"I'm sorry we can't do anything about it," the cop explained. "You're on private property."

"I'm a war vet and need your help!" I pleaded in desperation. "Can't you make him give me his name?" I insisted.

"I can do that," the cop said. He walked up to the guy's car and rapped sharply on the window with his nightstick. "Open this window," he demanded. The window slowly opened. The cop growled, "Give this guy your driver's license and insurance information." That did it. The cop stepped back to let me talk to the driver. The driver passed his license to me. His name was Elliott Blake. I copied it down along with his address.

"What's your telephone number?" I asked. He complied. "I need your insurance card."

"I don't have any insurance. Call me, Monday. We can settle this then," he slurred. I now realized that he was drunk.

"Are you kidding!" I screamed. "How do I know you'll pay? The police are going to arrest you if you try to drive out of here. Now give me your insurance card."

"We don't need to get the insurance company involved," he blurted. "I'll pay you cash for the damages. I've had a couple of accidents lately. They'll cancel my insurance if they hear about this. What do you say?" He was "beginning" to sound sober.

"This is not my car," I said. "I borrowed it from a friend. He's going to kill me as it is!" I sure knew how upset El was going to be.
"Try to make him understand my situation," he pleaded.

"I'm going to have a tough time getting El to understand my dilemma, without working on yours. If you don't give me the insurance information I'll tell the cops you're drunk."

"Give him the information," said a lady's voice. It was the first time I realized there was a second person in the car. He passed his insurance card to me. I copied down all the information.

"I'll try to get my friend to hold off contacting the insurance company if you call me Monday afternoon," I told the driver. "I'll have an estimate for the damage by then. By the way, you better not try to drive out of here. The police are going to arrest you if you do." At that moment, the policeman walked up to the car.

"I'll stick around to see that this guy doesn't try to drive again tonight," the policeman said loud enough for the driver to hear. As I walked towards the restaurant, the policeman joined me. "You did this guy a big favor. He could have gotten a drunken driving ticket and probably lost his license."

Back in the restaurant I explained my dilemma. "El is going to kill me! What am I going to tell El?" I asked.

"It wasn't your fault," Marilynn reassured me. "How can he blame you?" "We better all go back to *The Mansion* while I explain that to El," I said knowing there was safety in numbers.

El came home shortly after we arrived. I tried to explain to him what happened. "You wrecked my car?" El screamed. He went crazy. "You wrecked my car!" he repeated several more times. With the girls' help, we calmed him down enough so he could listen to the whole story. As El started to think more logically he said, "Mark, you take care of this first thing Monday morning. Get an estimate from a repair shop," El demanded. "Have that guy bring the check over as soon as you know the cost of the repairs."

"I'll drive the girls back to their hotel," El said. Apparently he did not trust me with his car.

Monday morning El drove us to school. "Mark, take my car and get that estimate," he said. I had prepared for this by checking the telephone book for the addresses of three different repair shops. I skipped my classes and went directly to those garages.

They were happy to furnish written estimates to repair and paint the car. The highest one was $100. That was the cost of more than five hundred beers. In comparison, the GI Bill only paid me $90 a month to go to college.

I telephoned Mr. Blake. "The cost to repair the car is $100," I told him.

"I'll bring the money right over. Give me your address." Mr. Blake, true to his word, brought a check for the $100.

"I only take cash," I demanded.

"I don't have that much cash on me."

"Let's go to the bank," I said. "You can cash the check and give me the money." I did not want to let him out of my sight. Mr. Blake agreed and he even drove there.

"Here's your cash," he said. He never even asked to see the insurance quotes.

When I picked El up at school, I showed him the three estimates. "Notice, the highest quote is $100." El studied the estimates.

"Call this guy and get my check," El said emphatically.

"Here's $100," I said, handing him the cash. El was astounded that I already had the money and pleased it was so much. "I hope this settles the matter," I said.

"You bet. I can't believe you got that guy to pay the larger amount." El said impressed with my handling of this affair, but he did not offer to let me drive his car again. I never told El that Mr. Blake was afraid that his insurance company would cancel his insurance if El filed a claim.

El was pleased when he got his car fixed. Little did he know that once a car is repainted it is never the same as the factory job. I did not explain this to him, either.

My third life lesson in college was how to handle automobile accidents. But what about finding a date locally?

The Survey

One sunny spring Saturday morning I was sitting in *The Mansion* feeling sorry for myself. Dick Heil, my roommate, was off somewhere for the weekend and I had nothing to do. No car, so going on a date was out of the question. All my homework was done. My laundry was clean and pressed. I did not know anybody from my school classes who I could call. My fellow engineers did not seem to be a sociable bunch. El and Tony, the other two guys living in our house always went on double dates together and did not have room for me. I probably was not exciting enough for them, anyway.

El came down the stairs after sleeping in late. "I have this job I promised to do for the University," he said to no one in particular, although I was the only one sitting there.

"What kind of job?" I asked out of boredom.

"It's a survey. They gave me this list of questions. They want me to go to this specific neighborhood and ask each household about what products they use."

"Are they paying you to do it?" I asked.

"Yeah, the pay is good—$10."

I quickly calculated, using my new and improved math skills, to learn that he could buy more than fifty beers with that kind of money. "That's a lot of money," I said. "How long do you figure it will take?"

"A couple of hours at the most," he said. I figured it would take longer, but it was still a good rate.

"That's darn good money. You should do it," I encouraged him.

"I just don't feel like it. How would you like to do it? I'll pay you the money myself. I'll even give it to you now."

I was not the least bit interested in such a dull project. My life was boring enough. So I felt safe saying, "How can I get there? Remember I don't have a car."

"Use mine."

I could not believe my ears. That was the last thing I expected him to say. The only time he let me borrow his car, I brought it back with its driver's side door caved in. After I got the car fixed, he swore never to let me drive it again.

"Here's the money and the keys."

Well, I'm already bored out of my mind so why not? I thought. *At least I will be driving around town in a nice car. Who knows what excitement that might bring?* I had visions of a beautiful girl in one of those houses. I might even find one willing to go out to lunch with me. After all, El has no idea how long this survey might actually take.

"Okay," I said, taking the money and his keys.

Parking the car, I started to canvas the neighborhood. It was not as boring as I had thought it would be. The people were friendly and willing to answer the questions, those that were home that is. But the neighborhood was not populated with sweet young things. That was probably because the people ordering the survey were not interested in what young people had to say.

When I got back to the car, I could not believe my eyes. Somebody had caved in the driver's side door, the very same door as the last time I borrowed El's car. I looked around. Who the hell could do such a dastardly deed? Hit a car and take off without even leaving a note! I looked up and down the street. There was not another car in sight.

Then the real calamity hit me. El is going to kill me! I could just hear El's Marine growl, "You - did - what - to - my - car - AGAIN?"

But that is not what happened at all! The first words out of El's mouth as I stepped into our place were, "Where the hell have you been? You have been gone more than five hours." That was the first I had realized how much time had lapsed since leaving *The Mansion*.

"You told me it would only take two hours," I said. That is when I realized I could blame El for all my problems.

"Not only did the job take <u>twice</u> as long as you promised, but I saved your ass in the process." He looked at me as if I had gone crazy. He had no idea what I was talking about.

"Some clown rammed your car door while it was parked," I screamed. "Yes, the same door as the last time. What is it about your car that people think they have to cave in your door? That's the second time that's happened. Your car is jinxed!"

El was dumbfounded. "You wrecked my car again? I can't believe it. You're the one who's jinxed!" he screamed back.

"Not at all. I'm the guy who saved your ass," I repeated, my raucous vocabulary being seriously limited. Of course, I meant his car not his body. "If you had been there, you would have cursed and sworn and probably even kicked the door yourself." I paused for effect because I knew that is exactly what he would have done.

"Instead, I went to work on the problem. I should charge you some exorbitant fee for my clever detective work." By this time El was looking at me like I had lost my mind.

"Here is how I solved your dilemma! I had been up and down the street working your survey and did not remember any cars passing. So where did the car come from that hit yours? And where did it go after the accident?" Again I waited, hoping he was getting into my story, rather than thinking about what he was going to do to me. I let that sink in for a moment.

"I studied the scene of the accident. There was a small puddle of water. Tire tracks led away from your car into the puddle and then disappeared almost immediately. The perpetrator had apparently passed through the puddle, hit your car and then pulled away. But there were no other tracks leaving the scene of the accident. What do you think of that?"

"What do you mean what do I think?" El screamed. "I think you wrecked my car!"

"No, about the puddle of water," I said. "If the car had pulled out of the driveway directly across the street it could have hit your car. But the driver must have pulled right back into his driveway. He probably never saw your car until he hit it. He then drove right back into his garage without going anywhere. What would you have done at this point?" I did not wait for him to answer.

"I went up to the door of that house and rang the bell," I told El.   May I use your telephone?" I asked the old gentleman who answered the door. "There has been an accident." He let me into his house. "I want to report an accident," I told the policeman on the telephone. Just then, I noticed the old man lurking around the corner within earshot. "It is a *hit and run* accident." "Give me the address. We will send somebody out there immediately," the policeman said as he hung up the telephone, but I kept talking as if he was still on the line. I began to build my case. "Yes, Sir, I can prove who hit me and where to find his car. The car probably has paint from my door on its bumper. That's right; the perpetrator is still in the neighborhood. I will explain everything to the officer when he gets here." I hung up the telephone and smiled to myself. As I started for the door, the old man came out of hiding.

"May I use your telephone?" I asked the old gentleman who answered the door. "There has been an accident." He let me into his house. "I want to report an accident," I told the policeman on the telephone. Just then, I noticed the old man lurking around the corner within earshot. "It is a *hit and run* accident."

"Give me the address. We will send somebody out there immediately," the policeman said as he hung up the telephone, but I kept talking as if he was still on the line. I began to build my case.

"Yes, Sir, I can prove who hit me and where to find his car. The car probably has paint from my door on its bumper. That's right; the perpetrator is still in the neighborhood. I will explain everything to the officer when he gets here." I hung up the telephone and smiled to myself. As I started for the door, the old man came out of hiding.

"The police will arrest the guy who hit my car," I told the old gaffer. "You know how they feel about *hit and run* drivers?" I expanded my story painting a bleak picture for him. "If I could figure out who hit my car, you can bet the police will too," I continued. The thought of my evidence rapidly disappearing, came to mind as I spoke, but I was desperate! I had to spend the time in his house trying to convince my suspect that the police could figure out just what happened. The old guy said nothing. The problem was, I knew the police were not going to do anything about the accident other than write up a report. "I'll just wait outside by my car until the police get here," I told him.

I dramatized my story as much as possible as I told it to El. "But back at your car, I found that the evidence had evaporated. I was doomed." I just left El hanging at this point until he was about to burst. Then I continued my narrative, "The tracks were long gone when I looked up and saw the old gent from the house approaching me

"'You know, I may have hit your car as I backed out of my driveway," he said. "I really don't know, but if you do not press charges, I will tell my insurance company that I did it."

Yes, yes! I almost screamed out loud. Instead I said calmly, "Okay." May I see your driver's license and your insurance information?" By the time the police arrived, I had a new story for them."

While I was waiting for you," I told the policeman, "This nice gentleman came up to me and said that he accidentally hit my car. I was nowhere in sight so he had to wait for me to show up. You don't have to press charges as he is fully cooperating. He even gave me his insurance information. The policeman gave me a look as if to say, *"What are you talking about?" We weren't going to press any charges.* I do, however, need a police need report," I told him. The policeman filled out the report on the spot.

"How is that for great detective work?" I asked El, as I handed him the police report and the driver's information.

El was so happy to see that I had solved his problem; he did not blame me at all.

"It's the same door as the last accident, but now you will have a new paint job," I pointed out. I still did not mention that collision shop paint does not hold up like the original factory job. Impressed with the whole story, El didn't say much. But that was indeed the very last time he let me borrow his car. The day's excitement was not quite what I had in mind when I was trying to relieve my boredom earlier in the day.

What Are The Odds?

I was hitchhiking home to Cleveland from Dayton for a few weeks of vacation from my summer job in 1955. A car stopped to pick me up on Route 42. As I opened the door, the driver, a well-dressed businessman, asked, "How far are you going?"

"Cleveland."

"So am I. Hop in." I was happy to get out of the summer sun and heat. After the usual introductions, including the fact that I was an engineering student at the University of Dayton and that he was a traveling salesman, I settled back in my seat. The driver seemed a little sleepy, probably from a hard week on the road. *Maybe I should talk to him to keep him awake,* I thought. I started my story.

"The likelihood of you having an accident with me in your car has to be a million to one." I waited for him to say something.

"Oh?" he said, seeming to be waiting for me to explain.

"I've been involved in three different car accidents in the last six months. I don't even own a car. You wouldn't expect me to be in any auto accidents. Not so!" The driver nodded as if understanding. Feeling the need to entertain my benefactor who was taking me most of the two hundred miles home, I told him my story.

"Last fall Jim, one of my roommates, suggested that we invite our girlfriends to the Homecoming Dance at the University. Neither of us owned a car. Our roommate, El, generously offered to loan us his brand new 1954 Ford Crestline Sunliner Convertible. He bought it when he got out of the service just before coming to college.

After the dance, we went to one of those all-night diners. While we were sitting inside eating, our waitress frantically screamed, 'Some guy just hit your car and he is taking off.'

'Call the police!' I shrieked in panic as I raced out of the restaurant. With the help of the police, I was able to get his driver's license and insurance information.

El was mad as hell when he found out what had happened. He made me do all the legwork getting estimates and collecting the money to pay for the damage. El was amazed when I got the guy to pay the price of the highest estimate. And in cash, no less."

After finishing my story, I waited to let my driver think about it. I wanted to see if he enjoyed hearing my tale. After all, he was giving me a ride home, which normally took eight hours and many different rides. I felt I owed him something. In the silence, I watched the telephone poles along the side of the road flip by. I could not stand the monotony, so I started another tale.

"The second accident happened when I hit a garbage truck," I said as I slid into my next story. The driver just nodded. By telling these tales the miles seemed to fly by.

"My dad bought a brand new 1954 Chevrolet. For him, a new automobile was a dream come true. He loves cars. Up to that time, he always purchased a used one because money was tight. I'm one of seven children." The driver nodded in apparent understanding. I continued."

"To top it off, Dad's car was two-tone, green and cream, very flashy. This was quite a departure from his normal color black, or should I say lack of color. To say it was his pride and joy was an understatement. His fellow workers delighted in razzing each other about the least little thing. This new car was major material for them to get on my dad's case. Leslie Kelly is my father's name. They called his car *Kelly's last fling*, thinking that he never would buy another car."

"'Leslie, you'll probably be buried in that thing,'" they heckled him.

"One weekend, while I was home from college, my mother asked me to take her on an errand. Returning home, I was driving down our very narrow street. Cars were parked on one side and a garbage truck was picking up trash on the other. I tried to pass, not realizing the truck had a huge wooden bumper on its front. While squeezing between the parked cars on one side and the truck on the other, I hooked that bumper. It did very little damage to my dad's car, but I felt terrible about it. My pride was hurt because I considered myself an excellent driver. Dad almost cried when he saw his pride and joy."

I let the driver think about this story for a while. He still did not have anything to say, so I continued. "The third and most recent accident I had in the last six months happened at school. El, you remember El?"

"Your roommate," he responded. "The guy who generously loaned you his car for the Homecoming Dance?"

"Yeah, that's him," I said, happy to learn the driver had been paying attention.

"El had taken on a job to do a survey for the University. For some reason, he just could not bring himself to do the work. He offered me the job and said I could use his car. The same car I brought back with the door caved in. And that was the only other time I ever drove it. Here El was offering to let me drive it again. Can you believe it?" I waited. No response from the driver.

"The money El was paying me to do the survey was good. It also gave me a chance to get behind the wheel of a car, which is rare for me these days. It was a beautiful spring day, so I agreed.

"I parked the car and started to canvas the neighborhood. When I got back to El's pride and joy, I could not believe my eyes. Somebody had caved in the very same door as at the Homecoming Dance."

As the miles flew by, I shared the details of my predicament and the super-sleuthing I used to unravel it. "El was so happy to see that I had solved the mystery, he calmed down. Impressed with the whole story, El didn't say much, but that was indeed the last time he let me borrow his car."

As the miles flew by, I shared the details of my predicament and the super-sleuthing I used to unravel it. "El was so happy to see that I had solved the mystery, he calmed down. Impressed with the whole story, El didn't say much, but that was indeed the last time he let me borrow his car."

"So you see why I say how lucky you are for picking me up," I told the driver. "The likelihood of you having an accident with me in your car has to be a million to one." I turned to look at the driver expecting some response. I was stunned to see that he had fallen asleep.

"Stop!" I screamed. His eyes popped open—wide open. He slammed on the brakes. I braced myself before the actual collision. He was unable to stop before hitting the car in front of us. I could not believe my bad luck. *Now I'll have to hitch another ride,* I thought. I got out of the car and walked around the wreck and stuck out my thumb. Fortunately, I got another ride before the State Highway patrolman showed up. Hitchhiking is illegal in Ohio.

"How far are you going?" the new driver asked me.

"To the east side of Cleveland."

"So am I," he said. He seemed pleased to have someone join him for the long ride. He looked like another businessman.

"Boy, are you lucky you picked me up," I said. "The likelihood of you having an accident with me in your car is more than..." I stopped in midsentence. "Oh, never mind," I said. *I better not make the same mistake with this guy. I've got to keep him awake.* I did this by asking him questions.

"What do you do?" I asked.

"I'm a traveling salesman. I've been on the road all week. It'll be good to get home."

"Yeah, I know what you mean. What do you sell?" Anytime he stopped talking I asked another question. By the time he dropped me off, I knew his whole boring life's history, but at least he stayed awake.

17.
A Nurse, a Midwife, and More
Dora Saber

My name is Dora Saber and I am of Lebanese descent. I was brought up as an orphan after, at age 5 losing my mother and my father a few years later. I was brought up by my maternal grandparents, and never felt a gap in my life. I had a good, happy childhood. I have had quite a few experiences and adventures in my life, which I want to share with my children, grandchildren, relatives and friends.

I graduated from the University of Beirut with a BS in nursing and then studied midwifery in London. I traveled back to Beirut by sea, which gave me the opportunity to visit a few countries and cities on my way back to Lebanon. Just before graduating, a friend of mine told me the company Tapline was hiring nurses at a good salary and accommodations. She was going to apply and asked if I was interested. I was, as I needed the money to pay off my student loan. I applied and was interviewed by the head of the medical department at the Beirut office and I was to start soon after, on July 1. The following experiences take place in Badanah, Saudi Arabia, a small village, in the 50s where I was working as head nurse and midwife with Tapline (Trans-Arabian Oil Company), an American company, of course.

Shortly after my arrival, the Prince of the district invited the camp superintendent and the senior employees to a dinner in his, so called, palace. The nurses and wives of invitees were asked to join as well. The dinner was, of course, the traditional Ouzeh, which consists of a large tray full of rice covered in mincemeat with a whole broiled sheep on top. There were several of these trays and we sat around them on the floor in groups of about ten. The way to eat was with our hands, forming a small ball of rice with a piece of meat and then throwing it into your mouth. I happened to be seated at the Amir's tray, facing him. Every now and then, he would throw a piece of meat to meat to me, which I was to eat to show my appreciation. One of the pieces he threw splashed fat on my dress which was silk and lilac colored. I loved that dress and this was only the second time I had worn it. It was stained and I would never wear it again.

One summer day a man came to the hospital from the prince's house. He brought the message that one of the prince's secret mates was in labor and needed help. The obstetrician came to me and asked me to go because a male doctor was not allowed to see her. He said to me, "Dora, be careful, she is small built and might need a C-section."

So, I went with the messenger and he led me to where she was. I was received by the prince's legal wife who took me to the room with a woman in labor. It was a miserable room and the woman was in a squat position. I asked her to lie down, but she refused, saying it was easier for the baby to come out this way. I told her I had to examine her and see how much she had dilated and how advanced the labor was. I finally convinced her, and she lay down on a hard, narrow mattress stuffed with rags. She was fully dilated and the baby's head was showing. I had to send the information to the doctor, so I went out to find someone to relay the information, but found no one. Finally, I went into a room and saw the legal wife praying, but I had to interrupt. She took my message and gave it to the driver, who returned with the doctor's response. He told me to do my best and try to prevent a third-degree tear. So, that is what I did.

I asked her to push and keep pushing as I used one hand to try and prevent a third-degree tear, and the other hand helping the baby out. Finally the baby came out and he was big, but there was no scale to weigh him, of course. The baby was dark as the mother was African I suppose. The placenta came out easily, but the mother sustained an unavoidable second-degree tear. I had to send a message to the doctor to come and suture the tear because I was not supposed to. The doctor, though, was not to do it without the permission of the Amir who was spending his summer in Lebanon.

The head of the hospital had to call the head office of Tapline in Beirut to find the prince and ask his permission. The connections were made through a radio system. There were no phones, and of course, no cell phones. The office in turn had to contact the Saudi embassy who finally found the prince and got his okay. The obstetrician arrived with the suturing set and whatever else he needed. In the meantime, I was taking care of the woman and her bleeding. Fortunately, the doctor had brought a flashlight which I held so he could cut the suture threads.

I bathed the baby and we left, but I checked on her daily. The mother had named the child Mutaeb, which means troublesome. When I asked why she had chosen this name, she said it was because he had given me lots of trouble when I delivered him. If a boy is born at night, they would call him Layl, which means night. She was very happy because having a boy meant she could stay in the palace. If she had a girl, she could have been out at any time.

When the Amir got back from his vacation, he wanted to meet the one who delivered his son and the doctor. An appointment was set and everyone in the hospital was telling us that we would be receiving a large amount of money or some kind of jewelry, but the doctor would just shake his head and smile, saying, "Yes, dream." He seemed to know what kinds of gifts were usually offered. We went and were received in a large nicely furnished parlor. The Amir stated his thanks, but never looked at me. He gave us both a watch. Mine was small, striped in green with yellow numbers so hard to see, I never wore it. Later, it became a nice toy for my children.

A few months later another message came to the hospital saying the legal wife had delivered a baby but the placenta was still in, so I had to go there with sterile supplies. When I arrived, I saw her lying down with one end of a string tied to her knee and the other end tied to the umbilical cord. This, I thought, was a very wise idea so the cord would not be drawn back into the uterus where it would cause a deadly hemorrhage. I kept the string tied to her knee and introduced my hand into the uterus and rotated it all around to be sure I felt the placenta detach. I removed it and examined it, making sure all the lobes were there. I was thanked and I left.

On my way out I saw a little girl sitting on the corner pathway, her eyes red from crying. I asked a woman who was walking out with me what was wrong with her and she told me that she missed her parents. I was curious and after some questioning I was told that she had been treated like nothing more than a "thing." She had come from a poor family and a man had bought her for the prince's son, who was only 13, to marry. She had come from a very poor family and was very thin. I felt so bad for the poor thing but could do nothing.

Tapline owned two engine planes and the pilots and hosts were Lebanese Tapline employees. The planes were for Tapline employees' transportation back and forth from the four stations to the Beirut airport. The four stations were along a line from Dahran, the main station for Aramco (American Arabian Oil Company). The Tapline stations were Qaysumah, Rafha, Badanah, and Turaif. They were named after the village's they were in.

The main medical center was Badanah where there was a hospital with doctors with different specialties such as orthopedics, gynecology and obstetrics, internal medicine, anesthesiology and others. There were male and female nurses, a laboratory, x-ray department, and a well-equipped operating suite. The suite had a general operating room, an orthopedic room, a delivery room and a cast room for putting on plaster. The other stations had only an outside patient clinic with a doctor and a male nurse, so serious cases, operations or certain examinations were sent to Badanah. The laboratory and x-ray department were headed by Lebanese specialists and Lebanese technicians. There were just a few private rooms for Tapline employees or a member of the monarch's family.

There were two large wards, one for men staffed by male nurses and one for women staffed by female nurses. There were three shifts of 8 hours each. The coffee room was next to the kitchenette where food was brought from the main kitchen, but if a patient was on a special diet, the Lebanese chef would do the cooking. The nurses and doctors had their coffee break in the coffee room. The outpatient clinic was on one side of a large, well-equipped room.

A bus would transport people from the village to the hospital. There were two separate waiting areas, one for men and one for women. The funny thing was that not all of them were sick. They came because they enjoyed the bus ride and visiting with friends they usually didn't have an opportunity to see. Every day, after the clinic closed, we would collect handfuls of pills thrown out on the driveway. They did this to show how sick they really were, and that they needed an injection instead of pills. They believed because getting a shot hurt, it had to work better than pills.

As you entered the hospital, there was a lobby surrounded by offices. The head of the hospital, Dr. Amjad Ghanma, Judy, the nurses' director, and the head of administration all had their offices there. The head of administration was a Lebanese man, who became my husband.

The other three stations had only a clinic with a doctor and a male nurse. They used the same system of sending a bus to the villages to pick up those who wanted to see a doctor. A dentist used to visit the station every six months to check the teeth of the employees and their families. A visiting doctor would come and update us on new inventions or procedures that were of great interest to the doctors and nurses.

When I arrived at Badanah, I was met by the head nurse, Judy Dunn, and was taken to my room in the nurse's house. The house was brick, consisting of a large sitting room, a dining space, a kitchen and four bedrooms. The kitchen was equipped well and had a washing machine and dryer.

We would often hang our clothes outside to dry, though, as it was almost always hot and sunny. But sometimes, particularly in spring, there would be sand storms, called Ajai or Touz. These storms were powerful, and if the laundry was hung out to dry it would turn brown from the sand. During these storms, the wind was so strong and the sand blowing so hard, we could not leave the house. Even with the windows and doors shut tight, sand would get in the house during these storms. We would put wet towels over our faces to breath, but in a minute they would be caked with sand.

The bachelor doctors had small apartments, two doctors to each. The married doctors and department heads had brick houses with three bedrooms. American employees with second level jobs had portable housing with two bedrooms rooms each. Other bachelor employees had sixteen by sixteen homes with two small bedrooms. No Saudis stayed on site as they would go home to their villages.

Expat employees of the more menial jobs would, if they were married, have to rent a house in the village as well. The houses in the villages were quite primitive and the wives of these poorer workers would come to the nurses' homes to use the washing machine or to iron. Sometimes they come just to sit in the air conditioning. Usually married couples like this lasted only one or two years before heading back to their own country.

There were many different offices at the camp such as public relations, office of the superintendent, the head of the pump house, maintenance hangar, and the canteen where we would buy our toothpaste, snacks, candy, and things like that. The recreation hall had a large dining hall attached to the main kitchen which was overseen by a Lebanese chef. There was also a bar, but they only served juice and pop. One of the American ladies asked me if I ever asked for a beer. I told her if I were to ask for one and actually get it, I would faint.

They had a movie theater where they showed newly released movies three times a week. There was a large hall for parties on special occasions like Christmas, Easter, Halloween, Valentine's Day and St. Patrick's Day. There were bridge parties on occasion, but mostly bridge and poker were played in the employees' homes.

The recreation hall was open to all employees, including the Saudis, who could use it anytime they wished. There was an eighteen-hole golf course and two tennis courts, but no swimming pool. Pools were prohibited until the mid-60s after I had left. Children, though, had plastic pools in their yards.

Golf tournaments were common and held at the different stations, so players would travel with their wives and children. I would often offer to babysit so the children would not have to travel. I would play in the tournament when it was in Badanah, but never traveled because of my nursing duties. Judy would travel for golf, and I was left to cover for her.

The housewives in the camp had plenty of free time and decided to start a woman's club with the aim of welcoming newcomers to the site. They particularly focus on helping new women, by throwing them a party and introducing them to camp life. The female nurses were always included.

The camp provided an elementary school for the kids. The school was run with American programs and overseen by the wife of an employee who had been a teacher. The superintendent's wife would assist. After completing elementary school, children would be sent to a boarding school, the American Community School in Beirut. Sometimes, American mothers would take their children back to the United States at this point to finish the child's education there. The teacher, Mrs. Hargrove, must have been of Irish decent because every St. Patrick's day she would be in green from her head to her feet.

A newsletter was started for the employees so people at one site would know what was going on with their friends and colleagues at the other sites. It covered birthdays, delivery trips, vacations, newcomers, illnesses and things of that nature. I was chosen to be the reporter for Badanah, so anytime there was an event, I went to cover it with an X-ray technician who was the photographer. He would always give me an extra copy of the photos, many of which I still have to this day. There was a time that Judy vacationed and I had not only the responsibility of being the camp reporter, doing my own nursing duties, but supervising the other nurses and babysitting Judy's dogs. I was happy to do it.

The hospital director, Amjd Ghanma, was married and had four daughters and son. His wife was a very sweet lady who kept a nice home, entertained beautifully and was an excellent cook. Her heart was open to all of us, particularly to the nurses. She was always there for us if we needed anything. Once, she suggested that she would love to teach us to cook or embroidery. I had always wanted to learn embroidery, so I asked my aunt to send me some good cotton material. I did two top sheets, one pink, the other the color of pistachio. I also did a tea set in light gray Irish linen which I used until it was worn through. The bed covers I used only once, and keep them now with my other treasures. All of her students did well and she was very pleased with us and very proud of how much we had learned. We were proud as well and showed off our work to all of our friends.

Their children were all well-educated and graduated college. The son had studied medicine and is now at Mayo Clinic working as an Orthopedist. He's married now with two boys and a girl of his own, all college graduates. In 2009, I was able to get in touch with his wife and told her I had some photos of her husband's family and wondered if she would be interested in having them. She said she would love to have them, so that summer when I went to Lebanon, I got them and mailed them to her from there. They were thrilled to see the photos. She said one of her boys looked just like his grandfather, Dr. Amjd Ghanma.

Besides sporting events, we used to have other recreational activities like picnics. There was an oasis in the area, and we would take a slaughtered lamb, make a fire and the men would cook the lamb and the women would prepare salads, appetizers, and desserts. The school children would accompany us and would have so much fun playing games and running in the open. The children would also take field trips to the hospital to meet the staff and sometimes even get to go into the operating room to watch a doctor apply plaster to someone's broken arm or leg.

The adults would have lots of dance parties. We would dance everything from the Charleston to rock and roll which was in fashion then. August and I would win every dance contest. In general, we were all very happy. There was no gossip, no jealousy or hatred towards each other. When any of us would travel, we would always ask our colleagues if they needed anything. We were always happy to get whatever they wanted, and we did it lovingly and more than willingly.

My aunt worked at a college and had summers off, so Dr. Ghanma asked if she would come to Badanah during the summer to cover for the nurses who were going on vacation. She had heard me speak about the place and life there and she was encouraged and accepted the offer. It was great company to have her with me during the summers.

Every year we were entitled to three weeks' vacation. In 1958, a few of us decided to visit the Holy Land. We took our vacation near Easter. There were two couples, and a male nurse who was from Jerusalem, but a section still in control of the Palestinians. We spent about five days and it was incredible and unforgettable. We visited the Resurrection Church, the Jordan River where Jesus was baptized, Beit Lahem where He was born, the road He walked when he carried the cross of his crucifixion, the large olive tree where He would sit and preach and of course, The Dead Sea. It was an unforgettable trip and we got lots of souvenirs. Other vacations I would spend between Beirut and Aleppo visiting my brother and his lovely family.

At one time an American employee, John, decided to spend his vacation in Beirut. When he returned, I heard him telling some other Americans how it was. He told them Lebanon was beautiful with lots of historical places to see, with lovely scenery of beaches and mountains. But, he said, you had to watch the drivers and the way they drive, "Every driver has their own God, and if the car had one more layer of paint, God knows what would have happened."

18.
Early Summer Mornings!
Jerry McKeon

Praise the Lord
For this glorious summer day
The flowers wink happiness
The squirrels at play

The grass as green as parsley
Billowy white clouds fill the sky
The suns a warming oven
For the whole countryside

19.

Fenced
Celia P. Ransom

My husband Jack and I have lived in our home for over forty years. When we moved to this house, the neighborhood was made up of families our own age. Every house had children. All our side and backyards adjoined, creating an open park like setting. Gardens flourished and trees shaded. There were no fences. We all had children about the same age. At any given time, we could check on them outside in the yards or through a window spot them playing. They were in and out of each other's houses. It was definitely a family neighborhood.

Time passed. Children grew and moved away as well as some parents. New neighbors moved in next door. They were a nice young couple. A year or so later a baby boy was born. They also had a big black Labrador retriever named Guinness.

One day our new neighbor, Mike, spoke to us of his intention to put up a fence. Guinness was getting older and had a tendency to wander. He noticed that the dog was leaving deposits in our yard. My husband said that he would rather clean up after the dog than to have a fence. I also remarked that when his son, Cameron, was older, he might want to throw him a football. If he told the kid to "go long" he would run smack-dab into the fence. Our comments convinced him. The open green belt remained.

More new neighbors moved in two doors to the west. They installed a tall wooden privacy fence. We learned that they had an autistic child. Their choice of a fence seemed valid, but it was a distraction.

Old Guinness, the lab, died. Our neighbors had another child, a little girl. The children grew and the family decided that it was time for another dog. Thus, another Labrador retriever named Foster came into the picture. Foster was an escape artist. The question of a fence came up again. By this time Cameron, their first child, was quite grown and by his body type we knew that he was not going to play football. The "go long" reasoning was not applicable. We had no redress. A shiny, new chain link fence went up. It kept the dog contained, but we viewed it with a certain sadness. We remembered different days and different times.

So now we are fenced on two sides and our panoramic view of lovely gardens and open space distorted. In addition, we are now forced to trim the grass along the fence line on our side. If this is progress, so be it. We still have our memories. But I wonder are there any more wide open spaces in neighborhoods today? Those open areas allowed us all to connect and watch over each other. Openness no longer seems a priority in back yards nor in life.

20.
From Poland with Love
Shirley Gach

My First Visit to Poland

As our plane lowered down, closer to the passing patches of green and brown farmland toward Katowice Airport in south Poland, I stared out the window—my knuckles pressed against my mouth, my heart racing with adrenaline and anticipation. I tried to swallow my emotion, but it kept coming up. That day, July 19, 2000, this granddaughter of Josefa Ruszel (Josephine), seed of her seed, returns to Poland, the land of my ancestors.

****

I knew little of my grandmother's early life in Poland—or why and how she came to America without her parents. When I was a child, my family and I made an annual summer visit to my mother's family in Allenport, Pennsylvania, where my grandparents had settled and raised their five children. However, my Gramma, as I called her, and my mother spent the entire week chattering in Polish—a language I did not understand. My Gramma spoke little English and I felt sad that we, therefore, were not very close. I guess it is fair to say that my Gramma never fully assimilated into her new country.

My earliest memory of my Gramma is when I was four years old. My mother and I boarded a train from Detroit to Pittsburgh in March 1945. I was to stay with my Gramma for three months while my mother started a new job.

One day, I watched my Gramma while she was praying her daily rosary—murmuring the Hail Marys in Polish and rocking on her rocking chair. Suddenly, she stopped rocking and leaned in to hear the voice on the huge wood radio that stood on the floor. She loudly called out something in Polish and began to cry terribly, wiping her eyes—and wailing again. She had just learned that President Roosevelt had died. It was April 12, 1945. She cried for a long time.

****

Our flight was just a few hours from Frankfurt. I felt so blessed to have been living in Germany for a few years—thanks to Phil's foreign assignment with Lear Corporation. Phil, my husband, always seems to know how to work in a business trip with a family visit or a vacation—and this trip is no exception. He visited a Lear auto seat making plant in Tycchy, about thirty kilometers south of Katowice.

Meeting Ryszard and Anna

My second cousin, Ryszard (Richard) Ruszel, and his wife, Anna, were to meet us at the airport. Richard's father, Walter, was the younger brother of my grandmother, Josephine. Richard and I had been writing each other for a few years and I told him we would be moving to Germany. We were both so excited that we would finally meet.

After clearing customs, we saw Richard and Anna with wonderful smiles and open arms—and we all hugged with tears and laughs. Richard gave me a bouquet of carnations and daisies—red and white, the colors of the Polish flag. Phil got our rental car with surprising ease and Richard followed us to the hotel where we would all have dinner together this evening.

Richard, 70, a man of stocky build, had clear blue eyes, a good crop of grey hair and a ready smile. He was an educated man who could speak and write in English which was how we had communicated the past two years. Anna has a stern face framed by curled black hair; she did not smile much. Anna spoke Polish and also German—a language that she was forced to learn as a child during WWII when the Nazis occupied her hometown in western Poland.

Now, I had been taking German language classes for six months, so I could speak and understand a little German. Phil, with his parents' Polish background, could understand a little Polish. While Richard took on the role of chief translator, our dinner conversation sounded like an international relations meeting, with laughs and good humor. All this made for an interesting getting-to-know-you evening!

Richard's Apartment in Gliwice

The next morning after Phil's business trip to Tycchy, we drove about fifty kilometers west to Richard and Anna's apartment in Gliwice, the town best known for being the home of the tall, wood radio tower which was attacked by the Germans in September 1939 and sparked WWII. Without a GPS, I carefully fingered the map, watched the signs and gave directions to Phil, who drove flawlessly through the rain, construction zones and through the city streets of Gliwice. When we reached Richard's address, we parked in front of the three-story, grey apartment building. As we entered, Richard came running down the stairs.

"Someone will steal your car!" He shouted with much conviction. "Move it to back!" We weren't sure that someone would steal the car, but nevertheless, Phil drove the car to a gravel lot behind the apartment building.

We climbed up two sets of stairs to Richard's second-floor apartment. He and Anna had lived there for fifty years, raising their two children, Bremen and Beata, who both graduated from college and became an engineer and a teacher, respectively.

The apartment was very small—three rooms plus a bath. The living room contained a sofa which converted into a cramped bed (as we would later see), a TV set, a bookcase, a coffee table and a coal baseburner. The kitchen was small but of sufficient space for Anna to make and roll the dough for her potato pierogis, to cook her cabbage soup and other traditional Polish meals. The bathroom supplied only a toilet and a bathtub which was used to bathe, shower, wash your hands and also for washing clothes. A swing-away wringer stood next to the bathtub. An outside clothes line was strung across their small balcony for drying clothes.

My favorite room was Richard and Anna's bedroom which also served as Richard's office—complete with his desk, typewriter, file cabinets and a bookcase wall that stretched from floor to ceiling, left wall to right wall—solid with books.

"Proszie! Proszie!" ("Please, please!") Anna said loudly as she graciously carried a chocolate cake to the living room and placed it on the coffee table which she had already prepared with a white tablecloth and a candle.

After the cake and coffee, Richard brought out a bottle of vodka, the drink of celebration (or anytime!) in Poland, and poured a shot for Phil and himself. The ladies passed. They toasted and Richard joyfully exclaimed as he held high the Polish tradition, "To Family! To Poland! Thank you for coming to Poland."

Letters from America

He then got up, walked to his bedroom-office and came back holding a five-inch thick, worn, brown folder. He paused and said to me, "Here, letters from your grandmother, Josephine, to her parents. When her parents die, she write to her brother, Walter, my father. When Josephine die (1979), her daughter, Stella, (my mother's younger sister) write to my father. But, he read no English, so I write to her. When Stella die (1993), her husband give my address to you—and you write to me. Here, all letters my father save—and I save—many, many letters!"

My jaw dropped. "Oh, my gosh!" was all I could say.

He set the stack on the table for me to see. I saw my computer-printed letters of the past few years on top, then I saw my Aunt Stella's hand-written letters on lined paper. Digging deeper, I gazed in awe as I saw my Gramma's letters written in Polish on fragile, yellowed paper. *What was she writing? What was she saying?*

Richard sat down and his eyes glazed over looking at my Gramma's letters. He reached for his white, folded handkerchief, wiped his eyes and said, "Hard life in Poland. Hard life in America."

I then took a deep breath and asked him the question that had been haunting me for many years. "Why did my grandmother come to America without her parents and the rest of the family?"

While showing me a paper with a hand-written family tree, Richard began, "My grandparents, Jacobus (Jacob) and Margarita (Margaret) Ruszel (my great-grandparents) had many children, eight children. They was very, very poor. In this time, America want many people for jobs and work. In our town, Lancut, (pronounced wine-soot) was agent from America. He want to take many people to America. The sisters and brothers of my father have not jobs. They made decision—we travel to America. It was very hard moment. Whole family wishes to stay in Poland—was very sad. They had eyes full of tears."

****

And so it was that my Gramma, Josephine, 20, left her job with the government railroad, left her family and left Lancut, Poland with her sister, Sofia, and a family friend who was paid to help them get settled. (Her sisters, Karolina and Anna, and a brother, Anton, also immigrated to America in the following years.) They left

Danzig, (Gdansk) Poland in February 1909 and sailed on the SS Bremen for their new life in America.

The three youngest children, Mary, Bronislava and Walter (father of Richard) remained in Poland with their parents, Jacob, and Margaret. They wrote letters to their parents in Poland and the parents wrote letters to their children, but they never saw them again.

Visit Lancut—Birthplace of Josephine

The next morning, Richard, Anna, Phil and I loaded the rental Fiat with sandwiches for a picnic lunch and bags for an overnight stay. Our plans were to reach Lancut in southeast Poland—a distance of about 200 kilometers—by two o'clock in the afternoon.

Although I had highlighted the route on a detailed map, Richard insisted we follow his better directions. Anna was always assuring us, "Wir haben Zeit! Wir haben Zeit!" ("We have time! We have time!") After four hours of missed exits, U-turns, deciding where to have our picnic lunch and Richard and Anna bickering in Polish, we arrived in Lancut!

A warm, sunny afternoon greeted us as we drove slowly through the main street in the modest and tidy town of Lancut. Richard directed us to turn right on a winding road that snaked through farms and yards and pastures. He excitedly pointed to a small white rectangular house and shouted, "There it is—house where your Gramma was born!"

Since the house was in the process of renovation, it was difficult to tell what was original and what had been added on to the house. The vacant house, which now belonged to distant relatives, looked like a three-unit motel. The white stucco house was long and narrow with three ground-level doors on the same side, a new orange tile roof and two new chimneys—one of them wide enough for a fireplace. A green lawn and trees wrapped around the house, but I suspect that a large garden of crops grew in that soil a hundred years ago.

I walked slowly over to see and touch the house—placing my hands on the white stucco. I wanted to feel its heart. I wanted to make a tangible connection to my roots, to feel the past and silently thank this structure for sheltering Jacob and Margaret, my ancestors who I never knew, and their eight children during those lean years and cold winters.

We all sat on two benches in the shade in quiet reflection— for me, trying to envision how such a small house could hold eight children and a mother and father, how hard their life must have been without plumbing, without electricity, without resources. Richard broke the silence. "In this little house live ten people. They had not good life. They was very, very poor."

Later, we drove a short distance where Richard showed us the freshly painted, two-story school that Josephine attended to eighth grade. He showed us the nearby 500- year-old dark wood church where the Ruszel family found the faith and strength to carry on and nurture their family with hope, where Margaret and Jacob prayed for their children—those who were gone and those who remained in their care.

Stop in Krakow

On our way back to Gliwice, we stopped in the beautiful, historic city of Krakow—taking pictures, walking through the marketplace and enjoying a drink at an outdoor café with many tables under sunny, yellow umbrellas. We watched the young people in jeans walk by—talking, laughing; young women with long blond hair—many of them squeezing a cigarette between two fingers, couples pushing a baby stroller, laughing children running and chasing pigeons...and the old people—a bent woman wearing a babushka over her worn and lined face; a serious, old man with

---

grey hair and weary eyes—sitting on a bench, smoking a cigarette and staring ahead.

Richard spoke his observations, "Young people don't know hard times we had—with Nazis killing our people, taking our land, Russians killing our people, taking our land, moving families. Young people study that in school, old people like me—we live it. We see it happen."

I understood his cynicism. In 1945 after the war, Russian soldiers, drunk with orders from superiors, violently implemented the ejection and displacement of Polish people from eastern borderlands. Richard and his family were driven out of Lancut by the Russians after WWII and re-located in Gliwice (in western Poland). The new arrivals from rural eastern Poland found it hard to adjust to their new environment and were resented in their new hometown.

Fortunately, Richard was an academic and allowed to attend the University of Gliwice and later became its professor of economics. Still, his life was carved by Poland's wretched history.

Leaving Poland

On the morning that we were to leave Poland, I was feeling humbled and grateful in spite of my cramped and lumpy sleep on half of the sofa-bed in Richard and Anna's living room. No matter. After all that I had seen and heard, I felt very blessed.

"Thank you" and "Dzienkuje!" ("Thank you!") were spoken again and again by Richard and Anna, Phil and me. "Yes, Richard, we promise to come back to Poland!"

We drove off. I was glad that Phil understood my silence all the way to Katawice airport. My heart was full.

Richard, Anna and Shirley

Richard's Bedroom/Office

The House

21.
Geriatric
Celia P. Ransom

Geriatric, does that term apply to me?
I did not think that it could ever be.
But of late, with no more color in my hair,
I think I have to give up and declare
That possibly others' perception of me,
Includes thoughts of frailty and/or senility,
And with my current white-headed block.
I hear "sweetie" and "dearie"; an answer that is stock.
Oh, woe, I 've passed the stage that used to be "ma'am."
And suddenly I no longer recognize who I am.

22.
Girlfriends
Sara Burnside

We're called BFF (best friends female) or pals; a girl's friends are priceless! No female with buddies would question a recent study that fund that spending time with them is as healthful as jogging. I don't know the benefits or exactly what boy companions do together. I can only speak to what my gender does on our play-dates.

I know it sounds boring, but my friends exchange the minute details of our daily lives. The frustrations of wasting time on the phone with any of the utilities, trying to save your pictures on your computer, a misunderstanding with family members or other friends, not getting enough sleep; are all fodder for sharing.

Of course, there are the times of deep sadness of the loss of loved ones, serious health issues or pain-filled disappointments that only our friends can help us get through. Their sympathy and support can be life-saving.

Finally, we must include the benefits of same-sex experiences that bind us. Finding the right hair colorist, dealing with an alien spouse, trying to keep communications with family members open, finding trustworthy house cleaners and repairers; the list is endless with typically female responsibilities that began with youth and continue to old age. Yes, guy-friends can have their purposes throughout our lives, but when I need an understanding ear, give me a gal-friend every time.

NOTE: My friends are younger, same age and very elderly, but all are invaluable to me. Our kinship has helped me persevere through job loss, parent loss, and just ordinary life.

23.

Gratitude

Al Rosie

Note: Some words intentionally misspelled

You want me to lend you ten dollars
That's a lot of money my frien'
What have you done for me lately?
That makes you think that I would give you ten?

When I got in at four a.m. one mornin'
I thought that my marriage was through
It's true I was out with a Blondie
But you told m'wife I was playin' cards with you.

But what have you done for me lately?
What have you done for me of late?
You haven't done a thing for me lately
So why do you figger that you rate?
That time I got stranded in Vegas
I squandered away all my roll
You wired me the room rent and plane fare
So I could get out of that hole.

But have you done for me lately?
What have you done for me this week?
Don't capitalize on our friendship
Or you might wind up way, way up the creek.

I remember when I got pneumonia
And couldn't afford those costly pills
You came ev'ry day to bring me comfort
And paid all my hospital bills.

But what have you done for me lately?
How have you helped me? Speak I pray
I'd love to assist you, old buddy
But you haven't done a thing for me all day.

You say that it's your anniversary
And you'd like to buy your wife a gift.
Believe me, I'd sure like to help you
But my money's goin' on a long shot in the fifth.

What have you done for me lately?
Why should I give you the mon—
Aw, come on, buddy, I was only kiddin'
Puhlease, won't you put away that gun?

24.
Green Little Frog
Renee Batenjany

Green little frog how natural you look, resting on the Lily pad in the fresh brook!

Green little frog how wet and slimy you look, jumping all around with bulging eyes, feasting on bugs as you leap!

Green little frog how beautiful your, rebit song is heard echoing through the air!

Green little frog how fortunate I am to stroke your head, for you promised to change my luck!

25.
Grief
Celia P. Ransom

Grief comes in a flicker or a wave.
You never quite know how to behave.
What can you do with leftover love, set apart
That still remains locked in your saddened heart?
Each day is much the same
A singular moment while dealing with the pain
Of love and loss...

26.
Grumpy's Testimony
Diana Kathryn Plopa

From the Desk of Max Ink, Daily News Court Reporter
June 14, Far Away Enchanted Kingdom Circuit Court Part Three

The bailiff takes his place at the front of the room and brings the people to order. "All rise. Court is now in session. The honorable Judge Fairness presiding."

The judge bangs his gavel. "Take your seats, please." He acknowledges the defendant and the plaintiff sitting at their respective tables, and nods to their attorneys. He looks to the defense attorney, "Call your first witness."

"Mr. Snide, counsel for the defense, Queen Anais, your honor. On this third day of due process, we call Mr. Grumpy Dwarf to the stand."

Mr. Grumpy Dwarf shuffles up to the witness box, his hat in his hand, and a scowl on his face.

Mr. Snide sidles up to the witness box, the pants of his perfectly tailored suit holding their creases perfectly as he walked. "Now, Mr. Dwarf..." begins Mr. Snide.

"The name's Grumpy, if ya don't mind." he says with a grumble and a sneer.

"Yes, certainly. Grumpy; as you've already been sworn in, please tell the court, in your own words, what transpired during the week in question."

"Trainspired?" says Grumpy.

"Yes," says Snide. What *happened*?"

"Ah... you gots some fancy words, don't ya, mister? Well, I suppose it started off as any other regular week. Me an' the boys were headin' off to the mines to dig for stuff like we always do. And when we come back, this... this hussy was in our house! Downright rude, if ya ask me."

"Is the woman you speak of in in the courtroom today?" asks Snide.

"Yes, sir. She's sitting right there." Grumpy points his stubby left thumb at Snow White, sitting at the plaintiff's table. He points with his thumb because he lost the first two fingers of that hand some years ago in a mining accident. It's only part of the reason for his sullied mood, but that's another story.

"If it pleases the court, let the record reflect that Grumpy Dwarf has indicated Ms. Snow White. Go on, Grumpy. Continue with your account."

"I ain't givin' ya no money, mister!" roils Grumpy.

"No, sir, not money... your account... your story of what happened that week," corrects Mr. Snide. He waggles his head in disbelief and not quite loud enough for the jury to hear chides, "where did they find this guy? He's a moron!"

"Well, like I said, we was headin' back from the mines, all hungry an' such, just looking for a little dinner an' rest, when that... that... argh!" Grumpy's face turns bright crimson and his beard prickles away from his face, making him look like a startled porcupine.

"Calm down Grumpy, sir. Just tell us what transpired," reminds Mr. Snide.

"Fine," he says, clearing the anger from his throat. "She came into our house, uninvited an' started rummaging around. She moved stuff we didn't want moved... ya know, cobwebs an' such. She washed the dishes that we'd purposefully left in the sink... no need for her to do that, we gots more. An' she MADE THE BEDS, TOO! The gall, I tell ya! An' then, she made us BATHE! I don't know who this harlot thought she was, strutting into our home as if she ran the place. The others... well... they went right along... swayed by a pretty face, they were. But not me. Oh no! I stood my ground. I told 'em, we can't keep her. She's not puppy, after all. An' for my mind, a heap more trouble! I knew somebody would be missing her an' come for her... an' wreck our lives even more than this one already done did. I reckoned they'd even come for the mine. But did the boys listen to me... NO! They just pranced around the house like Dopey, there... all twitterpated with stupidity. It was disgraceful."

"Then what happened, Mr. Grumpy?" cajoled Mr. Snide once again.

"Well, it was just as I told 'em... but they didn't want to listen to me, NO! Those ingrates... sometimes I think the lot of 'em is just simply daft. Stark crazy, I tell ya!" Grumpy was working himself up into a genuine froth now... spittle dripping from the corner of his mouth where he lost some control in that past mining accident... but I digress.

Mr. Snide enjoyed the theatrics of his star witness and egged him further. "Go on, sir... just recount the facts for the court. How did things change for your clan after Snow White entered your lives?"

"Well, as I said, the day of reckoning finally came. She didn't listen to us... let some stranger into the house... and BAM! Next thing we know, she's laying on the floor, near dead. I said good riddance to ya... but the boys... those foolish curs, they were smitten. Brainwashed, I tell ya! They actually wanted to put her in some stupid glass box to keep her forever. We're miners, for criminy's sake, not taxidermists! I just don't know what they were thinkin'. The whole thing was like making gold out of a box of rocks, I tell ya!"

"Please continue..." Snide encouraged, eager to capture his audience with the climax of the story.

"Well, that's when it happened," said Grumpy in a voice that was almost a whisper – quite the feat for such a crotchety old man.

Mr. Snide leaned in real close, his voice low and his body tense. "What, Mr. Grumpy, what happened?"

"We had to deal with... with... I can hardly say it..." Grumpy looked away from Snide, toward the townsfolk in the jury box. His face held the shame he knew was real.

"Go ahead," said Mr. Snide. "Take your time... find your words, Mr. Grumpy. What did you have to deal with?" Snide was waiting for the magnificent punchline he knew would sway this case.

"LOVE!" howled Grumpy.

Mr. Snide took a step back, eyed the jury with a heavily loaded pregnant pause, and said, "Love, sir?"

"Yes, LOVE!" bellowed Grumpy. "It's outrageous! We'd never had to deal with that infernal nonsense before. Our lives were simple... we went to the mine every day, did our work, came home, ate a bit, slept a bit, an' got up the next day to do it all again. We had a good life! An' then, this... this... wretched female came along an' made us all care for her! She wrecked everything! Bollixed up the whole works, I tell ya! Now, we had this woman to care for... an' she took her toll on us, I might tell ya! All that washing, an' proper table manners, an' making the beds each morning... It was ridiculous. We had a good life before she came...

an' then she went and complicated it all to pieces! The nerve of that woman! The boys an' I actually started CARING. ARGH! It's enough to drive a person daft, I tell ya!"

Grumpy took a moment to look around the room for some sign that he'd made his point... knowing that surely, there would be others in the courtroom who heard his plight and understood. Blank faces stared back at him. Grumpy went on with his story, hopeful that someone would understand and be on his side.

"An' then, when she was lying there, in that pretty box, sleeping an' such... well, I thought that finally we were rid of her. Finally, we could have our lives back. No more washing... no more cleaning... and no more CARING. But she couldn't leave well enough alone... No! Not this one. No sir!" He thrust his stubby thumb at Snow White again, punctuating his disdain.

Mr. Snide coaxed him again, directing the play with just as much intensity as he thought the judge would allow. "We want to hear your story, Mr. Grumpy. Tell us what happened."

"Well, this fancy pants prince came along and kissed her! Can ya imagine... the unmitigated nerve of the fellow... I mean KISSING a near-dead lady. Have ya ever heard such nonsense!" Grumpy spat his disgust at the prince who sat beside Snow White.

"What happened after the kiss, Mr. Grumpy?" cajoled Snide, again.

"Well, she surprised us all, she did. She sat right up an' kissed him right back. Then she jumped out of her glass box, an' said that we were all going to live with this Mr. Fancy Pants at his castle someplace farther away from the mine. What right did she have to say where we would live? An' we didn't have no say in it, neither. It's just wrong, I tell ya!" Grumpy's face again lit up like Rudolph's red nose, his whiskers alive with static electricity.

"So," interjected Mr. Snide; "she wanted to essentially kidnap you, and take you away from the only home you've ever known? Is that right, sir?" Snide had a cat-ate-the-canary grin on his face. He was proud of his star witness. "Grumpy sure is hitting this one out of the park," he murmured to no one in particular.

"Darn right, that's right! And she ain't got no right! I'm still the only one in charge of me... Ain't nothing gonna change that." Grumpy pounded his fist on the witness box, and looked adamantly at the judge. "It's criminal, I tell ya! Just criminal! She should be in jail or somethin'. It just ain't right!" The judge sat stoic... unaffected by the theatrics.

"Thank you, Mr. Grumpy," said Mr. Snide. "You may step down."

The judge banged his gavel on the desk once again. "Okay folks. We'll take a short recess, and return for cross-examination after lunch. Court is adjourned."

27.
Half Staff
Celia P. Ransom

Once again flags fly at half staff
This time for a young man loved for his hearty laugh.
At eighteen dying way before his time
Delivering an unspeakable sorrow for family and friends left behind.

And I can't help but ask why
So many young Americans have to die
Never to reach their full potential
Lives sacrificed they say for our freedoms so essential.

Yet when the struggle is done
And no one has truly won
Will we remember those young lives lost
And pray god at what cost?

28.
Historic Preservation
Jerry McKeon

I work out daily at a local health club. Along with my friends of a similar age, we call our workouts "Historic Preservation". This inspired the poem.

Look me over carefully
Do you find good "bones"
Can my body be restored?
Much like an historic home

As an older member of society
Brittle and out of shape
With a diminished lung capacity
And a muffin-top waist

Is it worth the trainer's time
To bring this body back to shape
To seek an historic designation
Before destruction is the fate

An older body needs cardio
To seal the designation
When senior folks work out
We call it historic preservation

29.
If I Were A Car
Jerry McKeon

As I get older with more miles on me
My body is like an old car as you can see
I have rust and blemishes on my finish
I move ever so slowly with my pickup diminished

My pipes are all clogged and mostly corroded
My body is worn, torn and bloated
A mouth filled with loose teeth with a bit of decay
And headlights that barely light up the way

My air filters are hardly able to breath
My shrinking body can't find the oxygen it needs
My tires are worn and beyond repair
As bald as the dome where there once was hair

There's one thing that still works as good as new
My exhaust is fine and the fumes it spews
Pollution has been cut with most cars on the road
But my catalytic converter (liver) is on overload

From time to time, my fuel lines need stints
My starter only works if you give it a hint
My mind is over seven decades old
It often must be told to come in from the cold

Often there's value in an old car
But not in old farts that's taking it too far
Although we're classics, others will grant
Our parts are not even good for a transplant

30.
If Life Was Without A Voice
Renee Batenjany

If life was without a voice!
It would be as a game full of charades!
If life was without a sound!
It would be life without a spontaneous music note!
If life were without words!
It would be life as a game of facial expressions!
If life was without a soundtrack!
It would be a challenging dream searching for the key
to unlock the music and sounds waiting to be heard
loud and clear with beautiful diction and articulation!
Oh, how incomplete life would be without a voice and
all that musical jazz!

31.
Italy (Keeping the Wine Safe)
Dee Trainor

Somehow or another, strange things seem to happen to me. Not bad things but unusual things; things that don't seem to happen to other people. Like Charlie Brown, I seem to have this small cloud over my head that follows me around wherever I go— not a black cloud mind you, but sort of a gray one.

As an example: Several years ago I went to Italy with ten other artists. We were going there to paint. Can you imagine? Painting in Italy where all the great masters used to paint. Altogether we were thirteen. Three husbands came along to chauffeur us around. Can you imagine a sacrifice of that magnitude? (That must be love.)

Upon our arrival, we rented two cars and headed for Gaiole, in Chianti, nestled in the hills of Tuscany. I felt like Audrey Hepburn and I'm sure I heard music from "The Pines of Rome" by Respighi wafting over the terracotta tile roofs of the villages as we climbed the narrow roads.

We pulled up to the beautiful villa we had rented. One husband got out and opened the gates... we drove over the cobblestone drive, past the swimming pool, rose-covered trellises, and colorful gardens. There were small, connected brick suites lining both sides of the courtyard. Each one designed to accommodate two to four occupants. They had a kitchen, bathroom, living room and two bedrooms. I was staying in the main villa in a room with a very low ceiling that nobody wanted. It was perfect for me, (I'm about 4'11".)

I shared a room with one of the couples, Dr. Dick and wife Eleanor. A small window in my room overlooked the courtyard so I always knew what was going on. I'm like that at home, too. I like to keep track of who's going to work, or church, or shopping, or the like. We ate in the open-air kitchen with a fireplace that took up one whole wall. The hearth could accommodate four standing people comfortably.

For lunch, we picked ripe tomatoes and snipped fresh basil from enormous painted ceramic pots stationed around the yard. We then added mozzarella balls, Balsamic vinegar and extra Virgin Olive Oil; and dipped the fresh baked Italian bread in the dressing.

Our sightseeing included Rome, Florence, etc. We saw magnificent sculptures, Michelangelo's *David*, the *Pieta* and paintings in the Vatican. We were in heaven. Back at our villa we set up the easels and did our plein aire painting right from our courtyard. A couple of times we painted right in the olive groves across the street!

A few days before our departure we went shopping in our town, which was only a few miles from where we were staying. Some were buying stoneware, service for eight, garlic graters made out of olive wood, aprons with pictures of the coliseum, and of course, we found some great buys on Violate, the wine tasting festival that was being held in the town square.

At the week's end we packed everything in the cars; easels, paint, brushes, canvases, and pastels (those were mine. We dumped the turpentine, since you can't fly with that, and then loaded the artists. Finally, we checked that the husbands had gas in the cars and the correct directions to the airport. With tears in our eyes we blew kisses and vowed to return soon; parting with an "arrivederci" or something like that. Then we headed down the narrow winding road back to civilization.

In the airport, we all stayed fairly close together and relied on Dick Gause or rather Dr. Gause, who seemed to automatically step in as our guide/director. We had plenty of time; we found our gate and just kind of hung around and reminisced about our experience.

One friend, Kathy M.; purchased three cartons of wine, four bottles to a carton. I didn't have much to carry because I use a backpack and a hip purse when I travel. I don't have many character flaws, but I do have one; I always want to help everyone. Maybe because I have been a single mom for years, maybe because I was a Special Education teacher, maybe because I always had to help my mom; whatever the cause, that's the way it is.

I offered to carry two of her cartons because she seemed to be struggling with them in addition to her other things. She's younger than I am and just as strong and healthy. Why was I trying to help her? It was her fault, buying so much wine, even when it was a bargain.

She is spoiled! She had a doting husband who does everything for her. She let me help her. As I walked along, the bottles were clinking together. Some people were looking at me but I thought, *Oh well, they should mind their own business.* It was time to line up at the ticket counter. I was fifth on line and Dr. Dick, a tall, good-looking gentleman who has a mild manner but was used to getting what he wants, was standing behind me.

The clerk looked at my ticket and said, "You're not on this flight, your plane is at gate 21 and is scheduled to take off in five minutes. You'd better run or you will miss your flight!!!"

I started to say, "there must be some mistake."

Then Dr. Dick stepped up and said, with a soft voice and a smile, "No she's with us, were all traveling together."

The clerk replied in a slightly higher register, "She's not with your group, her plane is LEAVING. I'll see if they will hold for a minute; otherwise she will be stranded right here in Italy." My friends began to mutter questions as the clerked picked up the phone and contacted the plane, my plane.

Dr. Dick was trying to reassure the others and remind them that there is a layover in Florence and we would meet there and all fly back together. I was in shock. I took my ticket back, picked up my, ah her, wine and start to run in the direction that the attendant pointed. I had to sort of squat down a bit to keep the wine bottles on an even keel so they wouldn't crash together and make so much noise or, God forbid, break and spill all over the floor. Remember how Groucho Marx used to kind of run low? That was me!

I don't know how I even found the gate. I don't speak Italian nor do I read it! The best I could do other than Pig Latin, was *Parlez-vous Francais* and I knew that wouldn't help. Or, maybe I should have said *Arrivederci*; but I didn't know what that meant either. I was shaking when I breathlessly arrived at the plane. They were expecting me and were anxious to depart. I climbed up the few metal steps and the stewardess took my hand, pulled me in, and closed the door. She quickly put me in the jump seat right next to the cockpit and clicked my seat belt. Within seconds, the plane pulled away from the ground and off into the wild blue yonder. My first thought of course, *was the wine safe?* Of course, I'm trustworthy. I had incredibly set it down between my feet. *Thank you Jesus!* I wanted to cry. I could hardly hold back the tears. The hostess sat across from me and just stared.

As we ascended she said something to me in Italian but I said, "I don't speak Italian." She seemed perturbed. Maybe I had her seat? She said in accented English, that after the seatbelt sign went off, she would find me a seat back with the other passengers.

I arrived at Detroit Metro Airport a few hours ahead of the others because of their layover in Florence. I was lucky, as I got a flight straight through, ALONE! *Should I wait for them? Hell No!* I was really angry by that time. I wanted to know who got the tickets. What travel agency made such a stupid mistake? I was furious. *No, I'm not waiting for those guys; all traveling together, safe, comfortable and having fun. The hell with them,* I got my luggage, hailed a cab, all the while keeping the wine safe and headed for home still feeling sorry for myself, *why me?*

After my shower, some of the husbands who were picking their wives up at my apartment began to arrive. Jokingly, I began to relay my sad plight. They were all very sympathetic. That made me feel a little better. You know, that martyred feeling is sometimes very sweet.

Remember Kathy, whose wine I was nice enough to carry across continents? Her husband met her at the gate with a bouquet of flowers because he missed her so much! I told you she was spoiled. I tried to get some compensation from the travel agency but of course, that never happened. In case you doubt the validity of the cloud premise, mentioned at the beginning of this story, I've documented other unusual situations, to substantiate this strange phenomenon. You probably wonder about Kathy's wine. No I didn't drink it although I should have, to teach her a lesson.

Karen, another artist who was on the trip, and I decided to meet Kathy at the South Lyon hotel for lunch so I could hand over the coveted contraband. I was glad to be rid of the responsibility. I could just imagine one of my kids coming over when I wasn't home thinking it was a gift for them, and opening and downing a bottle.

We really enjoyed ourselves, laughing and recounting the adventure. After a nice meal, we parted ways with hugs all around. On the way home driving east on 696, I said to Karen, "how much do I owe you for lunch," thinking she had charged the bill to her account.

She said she didn't pay the bill, "I thought you did! Oh no, call Kathy and ask if she had paid." Well, you guessed it; we walked out without paying the tab!! We didn't run, you'd think someone would have seen us and told our waitress. Well, we decided Kathy should go back and settle up, she lived the closest. She went pronto. The manager and waitress were very unhappy with her, but she's spoiled and knows how to defend herself from crises. We had a good laugh over that.

But they should have known better than to hang out with me.

32.
Joan and Mike's Wedding
Dee Trainor

I couldn't believe Joan, my youngest child, was going to get married and leave home. It seemed uneventful when the other kids left, sometimes moving in and out a couple of times before leaving for good. However, this was the end. Joan always said she was born in this house and was not going to move out until she gets married. She stuck to her word.

I harkened back to my wedding day. Almost thirty-six years ago to the day. July 17, 1948. The temperature was the customary 80 plus degrees. No air conditioning at Gesu, my church back then, and now at Our Lady Queen of Martyrs. It was hot.

I proudly walked Joan down the aisle. She said I was her mom and dad all those years and she wanted me to give her away. All eyes were on this sweet, radiant bride wearing her mother's wedding dress. Her wavy hair cascading down her back, then the long satin train following behind.

We met Mike at the altar rail. He was about 6'3" and Joan was 5'5". She took his arm and together they ascended the steps up to the kneelers in front of the altar. The bridesmaids and groomsmen flanked both sides of the platform.

I turned and took my place in the second row next to my parents. Behind me was the rest of the family. Jack, Barney, Tom, Patti, Pete and so on, down the line. Father Villeroit greeted the couple and turned, and the mass began. Epistle, Gospel, stand up, sit down, sing a hymn, stand up and sit down again; softly recite a few "Lord have Mercies", etc. Tom, my second son, gave the reading. It was a quote from Kahlil Gibran (Remember this was in the eighties.) It was something about your children not being your children, they are like arrows that we only have for a short time, and then we send them out into the world.

I was crying and wiping my eyes and crying and wiping my nose and crying ...

Then came the long awaited moment, the wedding ceremony Joan and Mike each walked around their kneelers and stood in front of the priest. Father Villeroit began talking about the importance of this sacred union. The devotion of husband and wife to each other, he stressed the Christian role of each.

Slowly Joan began to lean her head over on Mike's shoulder. It was such a touching scene it brought more tears to my eyes and I thought, *Isn't that sweet, get me more Kleenex.* Then Joan began to slowly lean more and more on Mike. He seemed oblivious. He was staring straight ahead and continued to pay attention to what the priest was saying. Then I realized that Joan was slowly melting down. I turned slightly to Jack behind me and whispered out of the corner of my mouth, "Do something, go up there." Then from the back of the church, my nephew, who happened to be in medical school at the time, walked up the aisle, as he passed me I got up and followed him. We climbed the altar steps and just as Joan was beginning to crumble, we grabbed her under each arm. (*Please do not slip on the long satin train.*)

We whisked her away from the groom, he never even looked at us, down the steps and, propped her up against the brick wall. The custodian brought over orange juice per the "doctor's" orders. After a few minutes, Joan began to come around.

This must have been a first because no one seemed to know what to do, so they did nothing. That had not happened at the rehearsal the night before! Joan had probably fainted from the heat. The beautiful wedding dress acted like a plastic bag, and of course, she had not eaten either, so she probably just got dehydrated.

After several minutes, Joan said she felt well enough to go back into the church. We helped her up, swung the long train around so she would not trip on that, and pushed through the large oak doors.

As we reentered the inner sanctum, it felt like a time warp. It was as though nothing had happened. The organist was still playing, the congregation continued to respond to the priest, "God Have Mercy." Mike was still standing, albeit alone, in front of Father Villeroit who was still holding the open missal and reading the wedding ceremony. Joan climbed up the steps, walked around the kneelers and took her place next to Mike, who was still standing and looking straight ahead as though nothing had happened. Then, not to miss a beat, the priest declared, "and now I pronounce you man and wife. You may kiss the bride."

The whole congregation broke into a thunderous applause and wild cheers. The wedding march commenced and the happy couple turned to face family and friends with heads held high and beaming smiles. They paraded back down the aisle through the high oak doors and onto the veranda. Everyone was laughing and congratulating the happy couple and throwing the perfunctory rice. Joan always says she is glad she got back to the ceremony in time for the most important part.

"What was that Joan?"

When the priest says, "I now pronounce you man and wife."

33.
Joy
Susanne Sack

*Written in the winter of 2003 after the birth of a grandchild and the
day after my daughter's birthday.*

The smallest of specks, dots, encoded strands join,
    swimmingly, inescapably, spliced.
The beginning: never to return to nothing.
    Forever the sky is split.
    The earth is graced.
    The reverberation of the bell sounds,
    the never before heard tinkle of giggle-joy cry.

Needs, wants, demands, never to be unknown,
    burst in.
Small, helpless, never to be ignored garments
    decorate the floor, walls, doorknobs.
Hours lengthen, time disappears
    never to return, never missed.
Time fills with heart-expanding,
    soul growing, color enhancing,
    twinking music of the spirit.

The body droops. The endurance wanes
The heart expands to near balloon stretch.
The joy scale tips.
When were you never?
We can't remember and never will again.
Welcome to the world, to our hearts,
    to our lives, to our vision of life,
    never again to be unchanged!

34.
Just A Man
Renee Batenjany

He is a man pleasing to my eye.

He is a man with strong trusting eyes and a cool smile.

He is just a quiet man with a natural and sensitive style.

He is a man with a dependable and helping hand.

He is a man with an honest look and a concerned heart.

He is a hard-working man with a quick wit.

He is just a lovely, delightful, pleasing man who has yet to discover me.

35.
Lady
Renee Batenjany

Lady with the weak and tired knees why do you hide your cane!

Lady with the sore back and large behind why do you hide your smile!

Lady with the swelled joints and the slow feet why do you push so far!

Lady with the large body and overbearing pounds why don't you laugh at it all!

36.
Lazy
Jerry McKeon

I'm lost in a sea of absurdity
Where the rules of life are ignored
Where rationalization and reasoning
Are routinely and illogically absorbed

A world where the truth is baffling
Where lies are for anyone to tell
Where a straight answer from anyone
Is to rise without burns from hell

In a world of tethered minds
And an equally restrained ambition
Ignorance is an excuse
It's laziness by definition

37.

Listening, Learning, Loving
Shirley Gach

I wrote and delivered this talk after the Memorial Mass at St. Regis Church for our son, David Gach, 27, BFA, University of Michigan. He died of AIDS in 1992.

I have found that LOVE, UNDERSTANDING, and ENLIGHTENMENT overcome all confusion, indifference and misinformation.

Eight years ago, I sought to overcome my ignorance of homosexuality when our son, David, told us he was gay. At first, it hit me like the proverbial "ton of bricks." My reaction was one of shock and disbelief. What could I do to help my son? What did my son need from me right now? LOVE, SUPPORT, UNDERSTANDING, YES! But, I soon realized that I needed to understand the "who, what, when, where and why" of homosexuality.

At the library, I sought to find the answers to my confusion and my questions. What CAUSES homosexuality? No one knows for certain. Some psychologists say it is genetic; some say it is environmental for a variety of reasons. NO ONE CHOOSES TO BE GAY—any more than one chooses to be right or left handed. In 1978, the American Society of Psychologists and Psychiatrists declared homosexuality to be in the REALM OF NORMAL, HUMAN SEXUAL BEHAVIOR. And, about 10% (or more) of ALL population is gay; always has been, probably always will be.

I came to understand that for many years, I had internalized society's and the media's portrayal of the stereotypical gay person. Movies, plays, radio and television—along with the jokes, have tried to establish a national image for those who are gay. But, the scheme is untrue. Homosexuality permeates the whole society—every profession, every race, every culture.

And, the reading was painful. I became aware of the DISCRIMINATION against gay people—their ISOLATION as adolescents, their STRUGGLE for DIGNITY, their search for ACCEPTANCE in a world full of INTOLERANCE, REJECTION, and INDIFFERENCE.

For most gay adolescents, their acknowledgment of their sexual orientation has been a LONG and LONELY JOURNEY with NO OUTSIDE SUPPORT. If a teenager is found to be gay, he is subjected to relentless name calling and abuse. A low self-image is natural as they have no positive role models.

Successful gay doctors, attorneys, teachers, ministers and other professionals do not reveal their orientation as a seemingly unavoidable concession to societal discrimination.

ONLY their sexual orientation makes gay people different from mainstream society. Basically, they want the SAME THINGS from LIFE that WE ALL WANT—TO LOVE and BE LOVED, TO BE RESPECTED and TO BE PRODUCTIVE IN LIFE.

UNDERSTANDING AND LOVING DAVID and his friends has ENRICHED my life and EXPANDED MY HORIZONS and my awareness of how I relate to ALL people.

If you know a gay person in your family or workplace, OR A PERSON WHO IS PERCEIVED AS DIFFERENT for WHATEVER REASON, REACH OUT TO THAT PERSON WITH LOVE. Let us celebrate the wonderful diversity of human life that God so lovingly created.

We can all overcome misinformation and confusion when we OPEN our MINDS TO ENLIGHTENMENT and our HEARTS to LOVE and UNDERSTANDING. And, like PEACE, IT BEGINS WITH YOU AND ME."

38.
Oh Sister
Renee Batenjany

Oh sister with the crystal ball, lucky charms, and a green glass frog, how funny you are!

Oh sister with the creative pen and paper, how clever you are!

Oh sister with the three children, one husband a pepper cat, how loving you are!

Oh sister with the leased car, large TV, cordless phone and new computer, how comfortable you are!

Oh sister with the mysterious taste, what a cook you are!

Oh sister with the supportive words, how lucky I am to have you at my side!

39.
Pioneer Jack:
Man in the Woods
Sheila Becker

Jack Mason has often been described as homeless. Nothing could be farther from the truth. His love of nature was so intense that he could not live anywhere else but in the outdoors. Jack was a modern day Saint Francis of Assisi, who was able to name all the plants, birds and animals that surrounded his home, a simple tent in the woods. Yes, this was his home, living amid God's creations, reading his bible, feeding the birds and animals. The birds and animals learned to trust Jack as we all eventually did. So this was the Jack we began to know.

At times he was frustrating. "Why won't you turn on the lights Jack," I would say. Jack would remain silent. He would never ring a doorbell but would knock on the door. Communication was through notes left on windows secured by duct tape. My husband went to ACO hardware store to get Jacks favorite brand "Gorilla" and of course in his favorite color, black. Signs of his use of duct tape can be seen all over our house and backyard. How did we meet Jack? Read on.

I am aware that in the Birmingham/Bloomfield area in Michigan many articles have been written about Jack Mason. However, I would like to inform all regarding my experience of where I first met Jack. Several years ago I used to take my two grandchildren, Julie and Jenny, to Pembroke Park, which is within walking distance of our home. Frequently, I saw this gentleman sitting on the park bench reading a book. One day I sat on the same bench with him and asked him what he was reading; so he showed it to me. It was the Bible.

We usually stayed there a couple of hours as my children loved it there, since it was a great playground with every child's play equipment one could wish for. I usually spent my time pushing them on the swings until they learned to push themselves. Now, I had more time to sit and talk with Jack, and to my great surprise, I learned that he was adopted at age two with his sister. His mom was a college professor and his dad owned his own computer engineering company. Jack informed me that he graduated from Michigan State with a degree in Horticulture, Later, he was in a car accident and I think he was diagnosed with a closed head injury. Jack did not talk freely about this. He drove a car when he was in school. When I questioned him about this he would say, "that this is an area I would prefer to forget" and became very reluctant to answer any more questions.

I asked Jack if he would come to my home and meet my husband, and would he like to help us with our gardening. He appeared happy regarding this. Jack came here and we agreed on three hours a week. Tuesday is the day he picked to work.

Now, when it came to lunch, Jack brought a great deal of herbal food, garlic, and special peanut butter. He informed us what he could eat; only certain foods, and eventually we were capable of providing that. Often, he informed us not to give him certain foods anymore like rhubarb, as it did not agree with him. Whenever he was here I always said to him, "Jack, take anything you need from our basement pantry," until one day I was not feeling well so I was lying on top of the bed when I saw Jack walking down the street with a brown bag filled with groceries from my house and returning empty handed. He informed me that he gave it to my neighbor. I immediately walked to my neighbor's home and informed him that we gave this food to Jack and my neighbor said, "He has been doing that frequently." I also spoke to Jack. From that day on I only gave him food to use for himself.

He was such a generous, kind human being. He used our basement to clean up and wash his stockings and would not allow me to put them in the washing machine or use my clothes dryer. Jack wanted to live like a pioneer, avoiding everything electrical. He would not open the refrigerator door, but eventually did after working here for almost ten years. During his time here people were very kind to him, much to my delight. When we first hired him, our neighbors were not very kind. They said, "We had no respect for him since he looked like a derelict." Eventually, they changed; that is the big reason I believe one should never judge a book by its cover.

In the last few months, when they did not see him walking past our house to Whole Foods Market, people were knocking at our door asking about Jack. They suspected that Jack was ill and gave us Doctor's names and phone numbers; like Doctor George at a nearby clinic, who would see him pro bono. Jack was not walking well anymore, he was seen leaning against the various posts and fences; his speech was garbled and he refused all medical help always answering to us that, " The Lord will help me". This is when my husband Jay would try to explain that through the doctors, the Lord will help him. People were helpful to him, like someone paying for him to attend the "Young Men's Society" where he would go and take a shower and use the facilities. When he was walking down Maple Road, a couple of months ago, someone stopped their car and gave him $185 saying, "I was in the same situation as you once in my life." When people saw him at Whole Foods, they would pay for his groceries.

My Own Experience With Jack

The neighborhood children called him "The Birmingham Bum" but Jack was not an ordinary homeless man, he was an organic vegan who wrote personal hand-written notes concluding with a "God bless you" to his friends and did odd jobs in a most ingenious way. This is my experience with Jack during the ten years he worked for us. We bought a special container for his tools and kept it outside, between houses. Next to this was a chair and Jack could be seen reading his bible in the nice weather. When my neighbor first saw Jack, he was scared of him as he thought he was a robber who broke into our house. Eventually, they became great friends, My neighbor has two lovely, large dogs and Jack used to give them doggie treats; and play with them by throwing a Frisbee back and forth; and they would bring their toy to Jack. He had a great time with their animals. He frequently asked me if we had more food to feed them. I had to inform him that their owners feed them special food. He checked that out with them and was satisfied to find out what I told him was correct.

Lunch experience with Jack was very interesting. He would spend a good hour over lunch as he had a very good appetite, He loved all vegetables, especially corn on the cob; he never would use any butter on the corn. For dessert, he liked pie and ice cream, but not rhubarb pie since it really upset his stomach. This was written to us in notes, which he taped to the doors or windows. Frequently, when we were sitting in the family room, he would knock on the front door. When we did not hear him, he would come around to the back where he knew we were in the family room, Again, we would say to him, "Jack, why do you not ring the doorbell?" We would learn that he would never use any electrical equipment.

Jack loved to learn Latin words pertaining to religion. My husband, Jay, would teach him "Dominus vobicum", which means "God be with you"; the response to that is, "Et cum spititu tuum;" it means, "and also to you". Frequently, he would get our attention by saying "I need your attention" then, he would recite poetry.

During the Christmas season, he was so happy that the family who allowed him to use his tent on their property invited him in for brunch on Christmas day. That was his first time being with Emily's family at her house. My husband, Jay, would play the piano and we would all sing Christmas carols. Jack had a very loud, booming voice, which was a pleasure to listen to, and frequently he would say, "I am so lucky to have my own home with the animals." I would inform him that, "I have had many a sleepless night thinking of you out in the woods in that awful snow and freezing weather", then his eyes would open wide and say "But Sheila, I love it" and I would not be content living in a lovely home like yours."

My children were very kind to him. One day when it was raining, Meg pulled over her car and said, "come in out of the rain" but Jack refused. I think he was in a bad car accident and that left him with a great dislike of cars. In the winter, he made himself a long plastic coat down to his ankles, taped with black gorilla tape. This had a large hood. To see him walking down the street, he looked like someone from outer space. He would not wear anything but black. Lots of people gave him good winter jackets, but they had red on them. He would not wear them saying, "I do not want to be noticed"; even though that plastic outfit that he made for himself was the talk of the neighborhood.

Jay was a great gardener; he planted an herb garden and Jack maintained it. He was able to name the various herbs to us and he identified them with sticks. Our neighbors were invited to help themselves to the herbs and took full advantage of it.

Let me explain the many ways Jack used duct tape; he only used the special type called "Gorilla." I found down in our basement, regular plastic cups taped; his special toolbox had tape on the handle; and whenever he wanted special tools or more tape he would leave Jay notes and tape them on the doors or windows.

Here are some of the notes he left us— Do not give me any more rhubarb pie as it upsets my stomach, (B) This is a note written to a lady who allowed him to keep his tent on her property:

Dear Emily, I hope you are well and prospering, thanks for trying to help me. I must inform you that I am a vegetarian (21 years) I only eat organic food. (C), at Whole food market, I buy 365 ounces of spring water, one-gallon organic, no salt peanut butter, and organic apple juice. (D) All food must be in plastic containers since the animals chewed on what you gave me; they opened the first container by yanking open the side. Take the water container out and put whatever you give inside. Water can be left out but closed tight. Thanks; peace be with you. God Bless.

Reverend Jack Brown, a former pastor of Pilgrim Church, was a great friend and mentor to him. He said the church took him under his wing in the mid-1990's. Jack honored the Bible, so whatever he did was biblically inspired. His joy and contentment was simplifying everything. He said, "He even tested my faith." Pioneer Jack Mason taught himself to say "Bless you" in seven different languages, and I know well that my husband taught him the Latin version.

Because he was intensely private, Jack's background was woven into tidbits gleaned by several in the neighborhood. He graduated from Michigan State with a degree in horticulture; however it was also said that he was in a very serious accident, which I think, left him like a closed-head injury. He declined all free medical help that was offered to him; like informing our family that the Lord will take care of him; and no matter how we would explain that Doctors take care of people through the Lord, he would come up with other excuses.

Jack's tent can be seen in the wood and the owner says, "I used to hear him saying the Lord's Prayer in the morning.

NOTE: Shelia and her husband Jay had a very special relationship with Jack for over ten years. They were one of a few Jack confided in, as he was very secretive about his past life.

40.
Puddle Jumpers
Jerry McKeon

Put a puddle of water
Just about anywhere
And then sit back
And fix a stare

At a school corner
I watched the kids
Come upon a puddle
Quite deep and big

The little girls
All walked around
The little boys
Behaved like clowns

They splashed each other
And tested how deep
They had to know
If their boots would leak

Stopping in the middle
Until girls were close
Then wet them down
With a watery dose

Puddles and stones
Are little boys dream
They just love to
Make little girls scream

41.

Renegade Dwarf:
Where is the life that late I led?
Al Rosie

High ho. My name is Sloppy. I'm a dwarf. That is, I was a dwarf until this bimbette, Snow White moved in with me and my seven brothers a few months back. She insists we're not dwarves. We're "vertically challenged little people". To hell with her! **I'm a Dwarf!**

Snow's been nothing but trouble right from the get-go. First thing she did was sweep the floor. The dust had been accumulating for a couple of decades and when my brother, Sneezy, got one whiff of the particles filling the atmosphere it set him off on a sneezing jag like you wouldn't believe. He's always been sensitive to the detritus from drilling the rocks in our diamond mine; but usually he's not too bad outside working hours. This Snow has to have fresh flowers in the house at all times. That aggravates Sneezy's allergies something fierce. He blows his nose so often, Snow has to wash his jacket every day to prevent a build-up of mucus on the sleeves.

My brother, Doc, was the brains of our operation until Snow took over. Doc even went to school for four years before he had to drop out because all that reading was affecting his eyesight. Now, he's blind as a bat without his glasses. The loss of sight was compensated for by a heightening of his other senses—his sense of touch in particular. Whenever he comes close to Snow White, his glasses fog up and he can't see at all. Snow doesn't mind—she calls him Feelie.

I almost wish I could read. It's pretty dull around here these days. I used to while away the hours sifting through my belongings in search of some particular treasure. One day, while we were off to work you-know-who came around and organized all my possessions, killing the thrill of the search. She calls what she did Feng Shui.

I'd like to Feng her Shui!! I'm starting to get things back the way I like them, but I'll bet the Inspector General will be making her rounds again in the near future.

I've got to admit Snow's not a bad cook. Problem is, she commands we wash our hands before we eat. Not me! I won't starve, though. She packs lunches for us to take to work every day. She told several of my brothers they need to lose weight, so they're delighted to share their lunches with me.

Since Snow started sleeping around, some of my brothers have undergone drastic personality changes. Snow recognized that by changing their names. Grumpy has become "Happy" and Happy is upgraded to "Euphoric". Bashful answers to "Tiger" and Sleepy is "Steamy". At least she cured his narcolepsy.

She won't sleep with Dopey, though. Claims he's immature and intellectually deprived, and she doesn't want to take advantage of him. He's not so deprived that he can't realize he's missing out on something. Now some of the boys have taken to calling him "Mopey."

She even hinted she'd sleep with me if I'd take a bath and promise to keep my belongings in apple pie order. Fat chance!

Speaking of apples—a hag named Queenie has been coming around of late peddling apples. Maybe Sneezy and I can con her into slipping a Mickey into a special apple for Snow White.

42.
Requiem for a Beloved Pet
Diane K. Bert, Ph.D.

When our cockapoo first joined us from the Michigan Humane Society, we began searching for a name for her. The first few days she trembled and wanted to be held, that is how we chose the name, Snuggie. As the months and years went by, many permutations of her name evolved as she endeared herself to us and we affectionately developed alternatives. She became 'the Snug', 'Snuggles Anna Bert', 'Snugger Annie', or 'Snug". Our daughter, Cherie, had wanted a dog for many years and Snuggie was primarily attached to her, although beloved by all family members.

From the very beginning, her lively personality brought joy, laughter, and occasional frustration to our lives. She was always quick to startle at any sound, running out of the room if anyone sneezed or coughed or moved suddenly, and barking hysterically at sounds at the door. She alerted us to sounds of car doors closing outside.

Any squirrel, dog, cat, or rabbit invading our yard elicited enraged barks from Snuggie. She definitely did not approve of meter readers or delivery men.

For many years, Snuggie settled down and slept in Cherie's bedroom. In later years, she chose a sheltered spot inside a closet. When this happened, a routine emerged in which we would ask, "Snuggie, are you there?" The *thump, thump, thump* of her tail against the closet wall was her answer. Laundry baskets full of clean clothes made fine beds from Snuggie's point of view. During the day, she would jump up on a bed, pull back the bedspread, place her head on the pillow and sleep comfortably. We often thought that she perceived herself as a human being. Perhaps she was encouraged in this delusion because we talked to her as if she were human.

So special were fresh vegetable treats that Snuggie would come running from the far end of the house when she heard the sounds of vegetables being cut. She would look up expectantly and dance with joy when given pieces of carrots or broccoli. The tough stalks of broccoli were the first things she ate when added to her dry food. We often mixed leftovers with her food announcing that we had prepared a banquet for her.

We would always get a grand reception upon our homecoming. Snug would greet us with joy and enthusiasm. Her unconditional love would lift our spirits and brighten the day.

In spite of our tendency to think of her as a person, Snuggie would revert to her basic instincts at times. We ceased buying rawhide bones for her because she habitually buried them in the potted plants, leaving great piles of dirt on the floor. Imagine our surprise when we spotted a peculiar looking lavender object poking up out of the potted plant. Upon investigation, it turned out to be a plastic bag of jelly beans which Snug had purloined from our daughter Laurie's backpack....Snuggie had not eaten any, only her teeth marks were evident.

More acceptable playthings were her squeeze toys. She raced through the house gleefully making noises with her toys. When someone accepted her invitation to play fetch or tug to pull, she joined in with whole-hearted enjoyment.

Her time with us spanned fourteen years. She shared every holiday. At Christmas, she had a stocking hung by the chimney with care. Each year she received treats and a new toy. One year her gift was a towel embroidered with her name on it.

In her old age, nineteen by human standards, Snuggie developed health problems. On her final walk in the neighborhood, she suddenly seemed unable to take another step and looked up imploringly. She was carried home. The vet assured us that we had made a wise decision when we chose to have her euthanized, sparing her the agonies of future problems. Through our tears, we did feel that we had made the right decision, although we felt great sorrow.

We still looked expectantly for her greeting. We still thought about how she would have liked the carrot scraps. We still looked up hoping to see her little black head coming around the corner. We still cherish all of the memories of her time with us.

43.
Seniors
Sara Burnside

When I glance at myself in the mirror (not often, as I cannot believe those hanging jowls I see!), sometimes think how much I look like my Aunts Pearl or Mary. We always said I favored my Mom's side of the family. Now I say I look like my Mom neck up, and my Dad neck down. But lately with my hair cut short, I think of how much I look like my favorite Aunt Louella, who is related by marriage, not blood. She and my Mom favored each other enough to be sisters, so this is reasonable. Anyway, as they have all passed, I am thrilled to remember them in this way.

When counting the pluses of getting old, (the minuses are unthinkable), and being called "Senior," one has to dig deep some days for reasons to get out of bed. The aches, pains, the frustrations, (I need not list them here) of daily life are sometimes unbearable. Also, the way modern youth treat the aged (either sweetly or condescendingly calling you "grandma" or rudely pushing you out of the way) can cause internal and external bruising. All are reminders that you have reached your prime.

But what are you going to do about it? (Aging, I mean) we may as well make the best of our end years and be glad we have them. After all, we have all those memories of great Aunts and many more we can count as pluses in old age. And let's not forget how the simple word "Senior" can mean discounts!

44.
Silly Clown
Renee Batenjany

Silly clown, floppy feet, funny tie and sore feet, how funny you appear!

Colorful clown, big red nose, frizzy hair, and bright eyes, how happy you appear!

White face, blue hands, sweet hat, are those hidden wet tears, how tired and sad you really appear!

45.
Simply Grand
Jerry McKeon

For those of us with grand and great grandchildren

Lots of things in life can be called grand
Maybe a grand piano or the grandstands
Grand Rapids and Grand Fork are two more
A grand slam adds four runs to the score

Being a grandmother is one of the best
Or a grandmaster in the game of chess
The Grand Trunk is the name of a train
A grand champion is the best in the game

But a very, very special grand
Is being an aunt to a joyful young man
In life grand pleasures are only a few
God blessed me with a grand nephew

46.
Slow Burn
Dee Trainor

As I look over my list of topics that I want to write about, I see that most are loaded with emotions. Some evoke sadness, some happy times, and some recall just plain anger and frustration. I guess that's life. The human condition! This falls into the latter category.

This story took place when my son, Pete was about sixteen years old. Pete always liked to work around cars so he got a job at a gas station up on Woodward Avenue. This was at a time when kids could get odd jobs. You probably remember where you worked when you were in your teens.

About this time, my older son Tom got engaged to Patti Heathfield. They had both graduated from Michigan State University the year before and were living in Indiana where Tom had his first job. Incidentally, I graduated with them. I got a late start!

Patti's family, her mom, dad, and uncle lived not far from me in Rosedale Park, in Detroit. Having a daughter-in-law from an extended family, I thought, would bode well for me. You never know when you may need to move in with relatives.

I had been invited to their home a couple of times for social gatherings when Tom and Patti went home. We also had a couple of mutual high school acquaintances. I thought I should have them over for dinner to reciprocate. I thought that we could become better acquainted before the wedding festivities began that summer.

This was a big deal for me. I was a working single mom and I still had kids at home. So my lifestyle was quite a contrast from theirs. If you read some of my stories you remember our house, it was even more worn out than before. Our oven door was still broken.

On the designated evening, I was scrambling around trying to pick up the house, set the table and cook dinner. I decided to serve meatloaf and baked potatoes. I'm not much of a cook and I didn't think I could mess up a simple meal like that—an oven meal that could be put on about an hour before company arrived. About twenty minutes before the guests were to arrive, Pete came in waddling like a duck and looking pale and scared. I said, "What are you doing home so early? You don't usually get home until about 8:30?"

He said, "Mom, I got burned."

I looked at him. He looked okay to me except that his pants were a little scorched on the inner thigh. And, he smelled like gasoline. Not unusual when you work at a gas station. In those days, the attendant pumped the gas for the customers. Remember that?

I didn't see any damage. I thought Pete was exaggerating. Maybe someone threw a cigarette at him and he got scared. Some people think it's funny to tease people like Pete. I told Pete to go to the bathroom and take his pants off. I filled the tub about one-third the way up with cold water. I knew that was the new way to treat burns. The cold water would stop the burn from going deeper into the tissue. Remember, they use to put butter on to cool off the affected area, but they learned that made it worse.

I told Pete to get into the tub and just stay there a little while. Of course we only had one bathroom. I hoped no one needed to use it.

When Pete took off his pants, I could see the inner thighs of both legs were scarlet and starting to blister. Just then, of course, the doorbell rang and in marched the three Heathfields. I explained what had happened and said not to worry that I had everything under control. A boldfaced lie!

I suggested Bob and Dick go into the living room and that dinner would be ready soon. "Make yourselves comfortable while I get you all something to drink." Actually, I was the one that needed a drink.

Catherine came with me to check on Pete sitting in the tub of cold water. Poor Pete, it was humiliating enough for me to see him in his Jockey shorts, but a complete stranger! When you were sixteen? Catherine proceeded to tell me in an authoritative, scolding tone, that I should be putting butter on those burns. But I knew I was right and stuck to my guns.

I told Pete to stand up so I could get a better look at the damage. By this time, those small blisters had joined together and become two giant sacks of water hanging down from his crotch to his knees. We were horrified!

What must have happened was somehow, a spark landed on Pete's pants and they smoldered. The fabric acted as a wick so it just burned but didn't burn up. Once he felt the heat he somehow put the flames out, not realizing that the skin on his legs had gotten burned so badly. It was a miracle his private parts weren't burned also. At least I don't think so. Just then, my nose reminded me that dinner had been done for quite a while.

I told Pete to just stay in the tub for a while longer. I assured him that everything would be okay. Another lie. I was trying to hold my own with Catherine, who was still nagging me to go get the butter. Also, I was trying to get Dick and Bob another beer. I didn't know it at the time, but I think I was multitasking before it became popular. I put dinner on the table and we all sat down. "Pass the peas please, pass the catsup please, etc. After a few moments, I excused myself to check on Pete. You won't believe what I found. While I was doing my hostess thing, Catherine had snuck the butter out of the kitchen; dried Pete off and then covered blisters with butter!!! Can you imagine this situation!

Here's my son Tom's future, mother-in-law, going unabashedly against me in my own home! A subdued argument ensued between the two of us. Bob and Dick didn't dare utter a word. I have no recollection of any dinner conversation. I was furious at Catherine and didn't know what to say. The damage was done.

There was no way I could get the butter off these two monstrous blisters. I just had to let nature take its course. After the company left, I got Pete out of the tub. When he walked the two sacks of water just sloshed around. I put Pete to bed with a plastic sheet and a couple bath towels so when they broke it would not soak the bed. We took Pete to the doctor the following day and Pete's legs healed over time.

The Heathfields and I became dear friends over the years, but I still remember Catherine trying to take over my responsibility and good judgment regarding my own family. I think the title of this story is appropriate; it states my situation just as it was, a slow burn!

47.
Small Town Girl
Sara Burnside

A sleepy town where people were reported to sit around watching the green grass grow. (So said a Scott Seed commercial.) It was true that everyone knew everybody and for the most part, we all got along very well. So constrained, that even as a kid, I imagined getting on a Greyhound bus just to get away and see how other people lived. It turns out, I did travel the world to observe other cultures, but this adventure did not mean that I wasn't happy in my little town. We knew each other and cared about each other. For instance, when I went away to college and returned for a visit, people I passed on the street asked me how college was going.

Reputations and appearance were important, too. Since everyone was in your business, so to speak, you wanted your business to be clean. I was an adult before I understood why Mom was insistent that my brother and I were home by dusk. Nothing good happens after dark, at least as far as teenagers go. Our family name meant something, so it was important to maintain that image. My dad owned an appliance store in town so our good name was important for business too. In fact, my dad saw no reason to leave our small town or county. After all, everything one needed was right there in Marysville, Ohio.

Now, just to keep the record straight, all this goodness did not mean my brother and I didn't enjoy some moments of less-than-exemplary behavior. I remember well sneaking into our basement one night past curfew. Mom never mentioned it, but I have a feeling she knew. Mom grew up as a Quaker. No cards, dancing, alcohol, were the commandments. Even so, I remember playing "Flinch", going to sock hops, and after a visit to the Holy

Land, I submitted to Mom that an occasional glass of wine was okay since Jesus himself partook. I have a feeling that Mom didn't know that roulette was a form of gambling since we had a wheel. All in all, it was a wonderful experience growing up a small town girl.

NOTE: I have lots of fond memories of growing up in a small town.

48.
Talk to a Senior
Jerry McKeon

With all of the new computer lingo being thrown around,
I used computer related words to describe an aging senior.

He's quickly losing power
His hard drive's almost dead
Hurry hit the save button
Before his floppy can't be read

This is about any senior
Whose story has not been told
There's so much stored in memory
Having lived to be this old

Long before their USB is shot
And their monitor grows dim
Long before their memory dies
And you can't count on them

Spend some time with a senior
Be sure to sync and take notes
You're about to get a history lesson
As this senior will connote

They will connect the dots
As you track the family tree
Failure to spend time now
You'll delete some history

They've lived in times past
Have seen things so resound
Don't miss this golden opportunity
Before their page cannot be found

Before a senior's memory is fried
And recycling will be acute
Converse with your favorite senior
Long before it's time to reboot

49.
The Case of the Infamous Wedding Gown
Dee Trainor

That title sounds like a Sherlock Holmes mystery, doesn't it?

Well, I guess it is. It all started in 1947. I had just gotten engaged to be married and was setting out to find the picture-perfect wedding dress. Remember, in those days a wedding was a romantic once-in-a-lifetime event. Every bride wanted to look like a virgin princess. Dresses were always white or ivory, bridesmaids wore pastel colors, never black or brown, and never off the shoulder. Also, there were lots of crinoline petticoats under the skirt. Anyway, it was a big deal.

There was a small shop on McNichols, or as we used to call it, Six Mile Road. It was a few blocks from my old high school, Immaculata, an all-girls high school where I graduated a couple of years earlier. The proprietor of the shop, Sophia, made all the dresses herself. As I sat and looked at dress after dress, she brought one out and said, "This one is special." It was love at first sight. I had never seen a gown so beautiful. It was an original.

It was a heavy candlelight. It had a five-inch wide piece of gathered lace that went down in the front, scooped up over the shoulders then low in back. The whole area was covered with a fine mesh. It was all but invisible. But modesty and proprietary were everything. And of course, this was topped off with a string of pearls. The long sleeves came to a point over the hands and had satin covered buttons up to the elbows. It was an unusual design. The bodice was fitted and came a little below the waist. Over each hip was a lace covered peplum, it has a Spanish flair.

If I had a fan and a rose, I would have looked like Carmen, the main character in Bizet's opera. The train followed behind for about seven feet. It was exquisite and the price was only $300.00 – that was in 1947. Then I came to my senses. "What!!! $300.00!" Can you imagine how much $300.00 was in 1947? But you know how women can rationalize away a minor detail like money when they need to, especially when it comes to buying clothes, especially a wedding dress!

But, I still needed a little support. I decided to ask my sister-in-law, Irva, to come with me and help me make the decision. Irva, my brother Dick's wife, was more comfortable with extravagant purchases than I was. Is that why I subconsciously chose her to help me? No, I don't think so!

When she saw the dress, she immediately fell in love with it also and said, "Dolores, you're only going to get married once. Get it?" (Do you like this 1940's thinking? Thank you Irva!)

The rationalization went something like this: I had a job; I had my own money; I lived at home; I didn't have any bills (this was before charge cards). And I didn't have any responsibilities. Besides, I was going to get married so I would have a husband to take care of me. (Again, 1940's thinking.) I bought the dream dress.

My mom made me a beautiful braided satin headpiece with little seed pearls clustered on each side. The attached veil floated down to just below my fingertips.

After the whirlwind of festivities and showers; a rehearsal dinner; and a wedding breakfast at the Red Run Golf Club, the big day arrived. We were married at Gesu Church, the parish where I had attended eight years of elementary school, made my first communion and was confirmed. These milestones were topped off with a honeymoon ay Mackinac Island. Settling in back at home, I had the precious dress cleaned and stored in an airtight box to seal in all the memories. Then up to the attic for posterity.

Every once in a while, the kids would take it out and look it over and joke about the old-fashion style. They had seen pictures of me wearing it in photos, but that was like ancient history. I don't think kids can imagine their mother as a bride. Besides, they had mostly seen me when I was pregnant, that is a long way from being a bride.

Sharon was the first one of my daughters to get married. She was marrying Dave, her boyfriend of about two years. When we started talking about the wedding, Sharon asked me if I had my old wedding dress. I said, "Of course." I was surprised she was interested. They were both working and paying for their own wedding so wearing my dress would have been a savings, and there was sentimental value. Also, Sharon looked beautiful.

She has brown naturally curly hair, plump cheeks, (we use to call her bubbles when she was a baby). Her hazel eyes and freckles completed the cuteness. Also, she has a contagious laugh and a sweet smile. She's only a few inches taller than I was, so she wore flat shoes. The dress fit her to a "T". She was a picture to behold; how sweet, my daughter wearing my wedding dress.

A couple years after that special event, Joan, my youngest child, met the love of her life, Michael Jack. Soon they were talking about wedding bells. They were also paying for their own wedding. It's a good thing they were frugal because right after the wedding, they were both laid off from their jobs. Joan starting flipping pizza at Little Caesars and Mike got a job as a dishwasher at Mavericks, a local restaurant. While making plans for the wedding, Joan said to me, "Mom do you still have your old wedding dress?"

I said, "Of course."

Back up to the attic to retrieve the special box with the treasured heirloom inside. You should have seen Joan in that gown. She has dark brown hair that flows in soft curls down her back about eight inches below her waist. How special is that, two of my daughters wearing their mother's wedding dress.

Lo and behold, a couple of years after that wedding, Carol, who had been living and working in London, England, met the dashing Mark Clewley – a true brit! They had met at a Rugby match. He was on the team and she was in the cheering section. Soon, another wedding date was in the offering. And then came the old refrain. "Mom, do you still have your old wedding dress?

I said, "Of course." Back up to the attic.

This was quite a formal affair. The waters of the Atlantic Ocean from the UK to the USA were churning with traveling guests. The groom's mother wore a large hat and carried a big purse. She was a dead ringer for Margaret Thatcher! The gentleman wore mourning suits and ascots at their throats. Carol, with her short dark hair and diminutive figure in this elegant satin gown with the train draped over the steps of the altar, was a picture of propriety.

As they drove off in a stretch limo, amid a rain of rice, both appeared out of the skylights waving to all the happy revelers. With nostalgia, I thought, *I really got my money's worth out of that dress.*

But now, I'm sorry to tell you, the story takes a morbid turn. All the happy memories associated with the enchanted wedding dress slowly began to evaporate. My husband left me after twelve years of marriage and later, I got a divorce. After two children and fifteen years of marriage, Sharon and Dave split up. Mike Jack was killed in an automobile accident only after four years with Joan – he never saw his son. Darling Mark Clewley passed away in 2002. From pancreatic cancer leaving Carol and their son, Tait, alone.

We used to think that some of the grandchildren might want to wear the wedding dress, but now we feel it's jinxed. We don't know what to do with it. We thought of giving it to a charity, but that seemed unfair. Some unsuspecting bride might fall in love with

---

it like we did and who knows what might happen. Hence the title, "The infamous wedding dress." It's old enough; maybe some museum would like to display it!

50.
The Gift from The Voice
Diana Kathryn Plopa

For Alan Almond; friend and mentor

On a night in early summer
He came to me in a dream
With the brilliant glow of moonlight
And a warm, soothing breeze

I saw him out walking
Through the woods on a crisp September day
He wore a cloak of magnificence
His horse was dapple gray

As we approached each other
He reached out his hand in simple trust
I opened myself up to him
Indulging in the enchantment, refusing to rush

We talked a while together
Exploring with wonder the depth of our souls
We walked on through fields of lilac bushes
And lovely marigold

We met there each afternoon
Enjoying the mid-day sun
Soon our hearts reached a place
Of blissful unison

He took me to his castle
Explaining he was a prince
Without hesitation, the drawbridge let down
Graciously allowing me in

On the walls hung beautiful tapestries
With rolling hills and majestic cliffs
When I discovered it was he who'd painted them
I understood further the wonderment of his gift

He led me then to his table
Where we shared a fantastic feast
Surrounded by the glow of firelight
As our quiet essence we released

He took me to his private chambers
And ever so gently, carried me across the floor
Together we visited such exotic places
As I had never dreamed before

Forever I will remember
The sound of his laughter in my ears
How his sweet voice carried me away
Vanquishing all my fears

As I awoke from my dream
I was elated to find
That indescribable joy and freedom
I had finally internalized

Today I carry his gift of enlightenment with me
As I venture through this constantly changing world
I am profoundly grateful to him
As my garden remains eternally secure

51.

The Hush

Diana Kathryn Plopa

When you touched me with your tenderness
Behind my eyes grew a well of tears
For the magnificence of your power
Opened treasures not revealed in all my years

The reflection of your spirit
Radiat4ed from just behind your eyes
The gentleness of your sincerity
Brought to me a multitude of starlit skies

When you caressed my soul with a whisper
Delving deep into the person I am
My entire body trembled with undeniable rapture
As your encouragement softly took command

Then you wrapped me warmly in a blanket
Quiet music and a silken touch
Your arms enveloped me as we drifted to sleep
Together we embraced the wonder found in the hush

52.
The Innate Flute
Diana Kathryn Plopa

The innate flute of society breathes assumingly
Its twisted mandate, quietly constructing
Their unrelenting doctrine; and insinuate
Him in this vast leg of their endangered
Journey... The core is presented;
Transitive thoughts; hate them happily

By night... inflatable revolutionaries mate
Starvingly... but by day, like recalcitrant
Icebergs, they preach unknowingly

Brave poet, codify simply this courageous
Socialism... Divide diagonally the wily
Blanket of quick fears

Inquisitive eyes quickly reach the
Twisted envelope, willingly defying
Authority

They open with anticipation the endangered
Doctrine... Finding only the largest hole...

Clean carpets carefully

53.
The Kelly Family
Mark A. Kelly

The Roller Coaster

On a balmy spring night in May of 1933; Leslie Siberia Kelly's truck plunged over a thirty-foot embankment just outside of Scranton, Pennsylvania. As a result Leslie, my dad, spent the next eight months in the hospital. My pregnant mother, Nora (O'Haire) Kelly, had to cope with this tragedy entirely without the benefit of income. The income had stopped as suddenly as Dad's truck. His insurance had been canceled months earlier.

Dad owned and drove for his own trucking company called Kelly Transfer. He rested in the sleeping compartment of the truck's cab while his companion continued to drive through the night to maximize profits. Unfortunately, on that awful night the driver, also, fell asleep!

During Dad's hospital stay, I was born to Nora Jane and Leslie S. Kelly in the insufferable August heat. Mother had to raise the family of six children; George, twelve, Rita ten, Betty seven, Frank five, John two and me. Fortunately, Aunt Katy, Mother's older sister, and Uncle Tim, one of her brothers, lived nearby.

Released from the hospital five months after my birth, Dad no longer had a trucking company or a job. It was the middle of the Great Depression, January 1934. Job prospects were dim. One of every three adult men was out of work. People stood in long bread lines in hopes of getting free food for their starving families.

At the time, we lived on Grovewood Avenue in a suburb on the far east side of Cleveland, Ohio, along the shores of Lake Erie. Our house had a three-car garage, built to house two delivery trucks and our eight-seater open-top White Company Touring Car. The garage took up the entire backyard. Later a brown 1928 Dodge four-door sedan, with wooden spoke wheels, replaced the Touring Car.

The finest furniture graced our home. The massive dining room table was supported by carved pillars for legs, and the chairs were too heavy for me to move until I turned about seven. We had a mechanical Victrola, which played recorded music whenever someone was willing to wind it up. We were the first in the neighborhood to replace our icebox with a General Electric refrigerator. Though we were very proud of that refrigerator, Mother probably missed the iceman's routine visits. He brought neighborhood gossip along with the fresh ice.

I did not appreciate how elegantly we lived on Grovewood Avenue until forty years later while on a tour of restored vintage homes. These beautiful homes were proudly furnished in the finest style of their heyday. Many items were the same as those we had had at the home of my birth.

My earliest memory is of standing in a crib crying. Through the window, I could see my mother leaving. She was taking six-year-old Frank to the hospital to have his tonsils removed. All I knew was that she was leaving me. I would miss her holding me in her lap, rocking and singing. From my window, I could see a box on wheels. Mother and Frank were getting into a horse-drawn milk wagon. The milkman was giving them a ride to the nearest stop on the Lakeshore streetcar line.

As Dad scrambled for work, my brother Kevin came along, in the spring of 1935. This brought the total to nine mouths to feed. Dad got a steady job at Cleveland Transfer, and things started to improve. Although for long! In 1937, the country was going back into a recession. Work at Cleveland Transfer once again became spotty. All my father's stocks and bonds had been liquidated. We were living from his savings and the equity in our home. By now, the family's finances were ruined.

When I was old enough to walk, Humphrey's Field became our playground. The treeless, vacant lot located just east of our home was a sea of grass. It was the size of three football fields. We played games and screamed our lungs out without fear of anyone complaining. No neighbors lived close enough to hear. While playing in the middle of this field one warm day, the sun was suddenly blotted out. I looked up to see a silver cloud settling over me. Fear propelled me home screaming. My father could not understand what I was yelling, but he looked where I was pointing.

"It's a blimp. It's a blimp," he screamed, as he ran toward the silver cloud. His shouts not only brought everyone out of our house but those of our neighbors as well. My fear turned to excitement as I joined the ever-increasing throng of people streaming to see the cigar-shaped balloon. It looked like it was going to fill Humphrey's Field. I approached the blimp, which had now landed; my father put me on his shoulders. I saw people in the gondola that hung below the balloon.

One of the passengers said hello to me. It was the Goodyear Blimp, known as "a lighter than air ship". The blimp had landed because the Goodyear Tire Company's picnic was being held at Euclid Beach Amusement Park. It was just across the street from my playground. The bigwigs of Goodyear had come all the way from Akron, Ohio, to join the party on the shores of Lake Erie.

When I was about four, I remember a truck making a delivery to the neighborhood store flipped over: spilling candy everywhere. That good news traveled fast! Children came from blocks away fighting for a share. We rarely got sweets in those days. If we did get any, it was penny candy. These were nickel candy bars. Baby Ruths, O'Henrys, Milky Ways and Clark Bars were lying everywhere. My first impulse was to immediately unwrap and eat the first bar I found. Then I saw the other children racing around gathering all they could get. I joined the melee. In pursuit of the loot, I fell, cutting my wrist. That was the end of the Great Candy Hunt for me. To this day, I bear the scar.

That same summer my sisters, Rita and Betty, took me for a ride on the roller coaster at Euclid Beach. We sat together, me wedged between them, in the front seat. Excitement increased as we climbed the huge mountain of track needed to propel the roller coaster through the ride. Peering down, the people looked like scurrying ants. Only when the car started down the steep incline did I become frightened. *"I'm going to die!"* I thought.

After a long, terrifying ride, I could not believe the car did not stop at its station! In the amusement park business, the second time around is the really big thrill! Once again we climbed that huge mountain of track going higher and higher. To my horror, we went over the top and again plunged straight down. I said to myself, *"I will jump out at the bottom."* But my sisters held on to me so I could not get out of the car. I vowed never to get on a roller coaster again!

Our dad's finances continued to resemble that terrifying ride I had taken. Unlike me, he could not get off. He was again experiencing a steep downhill plunge. His savings were gone, and now his equity in the house ran out as well. In the summer of 1938 the bank foreclosed. We were evicted. Where could we go? We had no money. And who would rent to our wild tribe of nine?

The Duplex - 6/1938

Dad frantically searched for a place to house his family. There were plenty of empty homes in our neighborhood, but he could not afford the rent. He followed every lead given to him by friends and all those listed in the newspapers. Then, God seemed to intervene. Dad located a duplex with one half empty. He moved our family just as we were being evicted. Somehow, he convinced the owner he could pay the rent of $30 per month. The owner, probably just as desperate as Dad, agreed.

Living on Grovewood Avenue, we were considered well-to-do. Now we were moving to the inner city of Cleveland. To me, the move was high adventure. To the older children, it was a disaster. They were leaving behind friends, school and all the things they knew for the unknown. I was almost five at the time, while George, seventeen. We had lived in that house on Grovewood from 1926 until the summer of 1938.

Our new home was located at 1591 East 40th Street, just south of Superior Avenue, and a few blocks away from Superior Transfer, Dad's new job. That saved him a daily round trip drive of over twenty-two miles. The owners of the trucking company, friends of Dad's, gave him as much work as was available.

Our new home had a picture window in the parlor, and a formal dining room with sliding doors which separated it from the kitchen and the parlor. The polished wood paneling and a grand stairway leading up to the four bedrooms were impressive. I shared a large bedroom with Frank, John, and Kevin. It had two double beds. I could not jump from one bed to the other; the distance was too great. Rita and Betty had a room of their own. The upstairs bathroom separated George's room from the girls. His room was small, but all his own. A second stairway led down to a large kitchen, pantry, and another bathroom. Our furniture fit perfectly. This duplex was a very large structure and in great condition. The neighboring houses were not so grand. Their paint was peeling and their picket fences were missing slats. People could barely afford food, let alone paint.

We learned that our new home had been the scene of a gruesome murder. A man had hacked a woman to death in our very own bedroom. A policeman walked the trial jury through our house, the crime scene, explaining it to them. The nightmares only lasted a short time for most of us, but for Frank it took much longer.

One night, the family woke to terrifying screams coming from our basement. Dad fearlessly raced down, followed by the rest of us. There stood Frank in the middle of the dimly lit room highlighted by a single naked bulb. Dad grabbed and shook him awake. He took Frank back to our bedroom with us trailing behind.

"Frank has painful boils on his skin, which makes sleeping difficult," Mother explained to us. We were sure it was fear of the murderer. I did not think I would be able to sleep that night, but I lay down anyway. The next thing I knew it was morning.

Our family owned one pair of metal roller skates that clamped to our shoes. They were adjustable so we could share them with our brothers and sisters. All that was required to re-adjust the skates to fit our different shoe sizes was a skate key, which we usually wore on a string around our neck.

Another family in our neighborhood had an uncle living with them who could play the mandolin. He often entertained us by playing lively music. He also invented a pair of roller-skates for his nephew. They were boots with five wheels mounted to the bottom of the boots, all in a line. Not like ours which had wheel opposite each other. His nephew proudly skated around the neighborhood in them all summer. That was the last time I saw "in-line" skates until the craze of the 1990's, more than forty years later. Little did we realize that we knew the actual inventor of "roller blades?"

The trucking company that owned our house used the other half of the duplex for their office. Their garage occupied our entire backyard. Many of the truckers owned motorcycles. We were treated to many a wild ride while sitting in front of an equally wild-looking biker. I would wrap my little legs tightly around the gas tank for fear that I was going to fall off every time we leaned into a sharp turn at high speed. There was also a motorcycle with a sidecar, which I liked better. It did not tip as much when going around a corner.

Dad loved to read the newspapers cover to cover. The Sunday paper was his favorite. One day he came running down to the basement where we were playing. "See this man?" he said, showing us a magnificently colored drawing of a British Army Officer in India wearing a pith helmet and full uniform. The officer, standing on a hillside striking a military pose, presented a powerful image to us. "I knew this man back in England," Dad proclaimed. "When I was a lad of ten he came to town campaigning for a seat in the British Parliament. In those days, the politicians used the local schoolhouses as gathering places to make speeches. He did not know where they were located. He needed a guide. My family owned a general store and we delivered the larger pieces of furniture by a horse drawn wagon. I went along on those deliveries so I knew the territory."

That may explain why my father started a package delivery service of his own once he came to the U.S. He already knew the delivery business. "My father volunteered my services," Dad continued his story. "The man's name is George Lloyd. He is now the Viceroy of India."

"I thought you said he was Prime Minister of England," Frank said.

"No, that was another man named Lloyd George. This is George Lloyd, but I'm impressed that you remembered that," Dad praised Frank. Dad continued his story. "George Lloyd owned a long magnificent automobile. The chauffeur sat in an open-top front seat of shiny leather while the owner sat in a closed compartment in back. The car was polished black with gold trim. The headlights were as big as that water pail," he said, pointing at a bucket sitting in the corner. "I sat up front and directed the chauffeur to the various schools. I vowed to own an automobile too someday. You are more likely to own an airplane in your lifetime than I was to own an automobile," Dad said.

Up until that time, I had only seen a half-dozen airplanes flying overhead. They were skywriting advertisements for Coca-Cola or Pepsi-Cola. I was never going to own an airplane, yet my father had already owned two automobiles to my knowledge. *"Maybe I will own an airplane someday,"* I thought to myself. That set my mind reeling.

I have many memories about playing in the duplex. It was a very large house with two separate stairways leading to the long hallway upstairs. The largest room in our house was the attic. It seemed as large as a ballroom to me.

Leslie S Kelly – 11/3/1896 – 12/11/1984

My father, Leslie Siberia Kelly, was born November 3, 1896, to a wealthy family in the town of Newport in Shropshire, England. He was the eldest of seven children. When his mother, Jane Thurstfield, died in childbirth after only fourteen years of marriage, Grandfather Frank married again. He needed someone to help raise his brood. The new wife was soon on her way to having a brood of her own - seven more children. She resented the work involved in raising the first family and complained constantly about their disrespect towards her.

World War I broke out between England and Germany in the summer of 1914. It was only a matter of time before a seventeen - year-old, Leslie could be drafted. His father did not want that to happen. Also, it was an excuse to lessen his family of fourteen by one. The stepmother liked that. To avoid being drafted Leslie's father booked him passage on the steamship, the *Cedric*, bound for the United States. He was given money for his expenses and the name of a family friend in Cleveland, Ohio, who could help get him started in the new country. My father, Leslie Kelly landed on the American shore August 11, 1914.

Within a year, Leslie was traveling across the country as a hobo. Hobos were a collection of destitute bums, drifters, vagabonds and homeless tramps who usually traveled by freight trains going from one camp to another. These camps were located near the freight train terminals of large cities across the country. These drifters gathered around a fire and cooked whatever food they could find or steal. They did not dare build a makeshift city of boxes or tents. This gave their location away to the railroad police, their sworn enemies, known as "railroad dicks." When it came time to move on, usually because of pressure from the "dicks," they hopped aboard an empty boxcar of any slow moving train leaving the freight yard. This method of travel was called "riding the rails." Dad joined the hobos to see the country. It was his way to travel free and go anywhere. Dad covered the entire country from east to west and back again over a year's time.

While laying around a campfire out west, the hobos were approached by a farmer with an offer of employment. "I've got some crops to bring in if any of you are willing to put in a good day's work for a good day's pay. I will even throw in meals," he offered.

"Is it nice rolling countryside?" one of the reclining bums asked the farmer.

"Why, yes it is," he answered enthusiastically.

"Then roll it down here and we'll take a look," the bum said.

"Ah, you guys don't want to work," said the disgusted farmer. The bums jeered him as he walked away.

As the U.S. got involved in the war effort, Dad found employment with The White Motor Company, makers of trucks and fire engines. He was delivering a fire engine to an Army base when the terrible influenza epidemic of 1917-1919 broke out.

"The ambulances were lined up at the hospital waiting for the soldiers to die." Dad explained to me how bad the situation had grown. "Everyone was confined to the base. I feared for my life so I snuck away!" Luckily, he did not get sick and spread the dreaded disease. It eventually killed twenty to thirty million people worldwide.

Dad's job at The White Motor Company developed into an important position. He became the expert on fire engines that had their own water pumping system. The fire engines were delivered by railway car. Dad rode on the same train and supervised the unloading of the engines and the training of the fire department.

"It was a big happening for the city or village when the new fire engine was delivered," Dad said. "Some prominent citizen had usually donated it and the city organized a picnic around its delivery. The entire town gathered for the party. Free food and drink was provided for all. The high point of the celebration was when the announcement was made that the demonstration was about to begin."

"I parked the truck next to the lake or pond at the picnic area," Dad told me. "When the crowd gathered around the fire truck, I unrolled the suction hose and dropped it into the lake. I revved the engine and flipped the pump switch. The water from the hose shot high into the air. The crowd was momentarily struck dumb, and then they cheered wildly. It was the equivalent of a 4th of July fireworks display," Dad said, ending his story. He liked to think of himself as the hero of those festivities and he loved that!

Twenty-five years later while on a family vacation traveling through the South with Mother, Dad, John and Kevin, we found ourselves in a small town whose name I did not recognize. As navigator for these trips, I did not understand why Dad asked me to direct us to some burg off the main route to our Florida destination.

"I delivered a fire engine here once in the old days," Dad explained. Sure enough, he found some old codger who remembered that event long ago, when the town took delivery of their first fire truck. Dad spent hours talking to the townspeople, reliving his glory days, while we sat and baked in our car.

In Dad's glory days, balloon tires came into vogue. White Motor was still delivering new trucks to the sales delivery depot with solid rubber tires on them. People who were buying a new truck wanted the latest equipment, none of those solid rubber things. To satisfy their customers, the sales manager bought balloon tires from a local supplier and swapped them. The depot's back lot soon overflowed with solid rubber tires removed from the trucks before they were sold.

"What're we going to do with all these useless tires?" the sales manager asked Dad.

"How much will you take for them?" Dad asked as he formulated a plan.

"Five dollars apiece," said his boss. "After all, they are useless. I just want to get them out of here!"

Dad set about finding a market for those tires. There turned out to be a great demand for solid rubber tires. Truckers who needed replacement tires for their existing vehicles could not always afford the new balloon ones. Tires were very expensive - even solid-rubber ones. Dad sold them all, some for as much as seventy-five dollars apiece; but he only paid White Motor the required five dollars. He pocketed the difference. At first, the sales manager was pleased to be getting them out of his way, but he became jealous that Dad was making all that extra money. About this time, the sales manager's son needed a job. Dad's boss used this as an excuse to fire him and hire his own son. Dad had to look for a new job.

In those days, people did most of their shopping, other than for food, at downtown department stores. They traveled to these stores by public transportation called streetcars. The major stores realized the limitations on how many purchases these people could carry home. They offered a free service to deliver these packages to the customer's homes. That encouraged shoppers to buy more. The stores operated their own fleet of delivery trucks, but smaller stores could not afford to do this. Dad approached these smaller stores with an offer to deliver their packages for an attractive price. Before long, Dad owned two trucks that covered the entire city. *Kelly Delivery* was a lucrative business.

The business was so profitable that soon it invited a competitor. Rather than continue the battle, Dad proposed to buy out the competition or have them buy his company. They bought his company. Once again it was time to look for new employment.

There was big money to be made delivering goods from Cleveland to New York City. Dad started a company call *Kelly Transfer* for "over the road" hauling. Rather than returning from New York with an empty truck, as did others in the business, he solicited companies in New York that needed their goods delivered to Cleveland on his return trip.

He purchased a truck called a semi, which could pull a separate trailer. In the cab of this truck was a sleeping compartment behind the driver. By using two drivers, he was able to keep the truck moving night and day. He proved to be right again and the family business prospered even more.

His troubles began when he added a second semi. This required another set of drivers. One of these drivers, Clarence, had several accidents through his carelessness, which caused the insurance company to cancel Dad's coverage. Dad took Clarence with him when he went to talk to the insurance company.

"See this man?" he said to the insurance agent, pointing towards Clarence, "He is the cause of all those accidents. He is going to kill himself someday. Therefore, I am firing him here and now. He will never drive a truck for me again!"

Despite Dad's plea, the insurance company did not reinstate Dad's insurance coverage. The irony is that later, Clarence did get killed through his own negligence. While inspecting the tires of the truck he was to drive, he stepped into the path of an oncoming truck and was killed instantly.

Dad found part-time work with *Cleveland Transfer*, the company that had purchased his package delivery business. It was temporary work. With time on his hands, Dad became involved in the truck driver's union movement. This was a dangerous thing to do in those days. Dad enjoyed telling horror stories about beating and being beaten by company thugs.

During this period, Baby Face Nelson, a notorious gangster of the day, accosted Dad. While being chased by the police, Baby Face jumped on the running board of Dad's truck, gun in hand. He directed Dad to drive him to his waiting car. Miraculously, the gangster got away and Dad was not hurt.

Dad thought he was in control of every part of his life. He believed all he had to do was be smart and work hard. He did not understand how little control we have over our own lives. After building two successful businesses, he found himself completely broke.

Things definitely were not going well for him. Making enough money to feed the family was a constant challenge. Under the financial strain, Dad often took out his frustrations on Mother and us kids.

"If it weren't for the Church I wouldn't have all these damned kids to feed," he said. He blamed the Catholic Church for everything. "You give them all my money," he accused Mother. She did give her money away, but not always to the Church!

NORA JANE HAIRE - 11/26/1895 to 9/12/1971

My Mother's relatives lived in Ireland. In 1850, Michael Haire, her grandfather, married Catherine Monaghan, the local schoolmistress. Catherine was a highly regarded professional. The fact that she was educated added to the family's prestige. Her family owned a hotel in Cornmarket, Ballinrobe, in County Mayo. Michael and Catherine ran a thriving bakery on Main Street in Ballinrobe. They had four children: Michael Jr., William, Katie, and Monica. Michael Jr. later became my mother's father.

When Michael Sr. died, Catherine, now without a husband, set about securing her family's future. A thirty-acre farm in Bunnadubber, Ballinrobe owned by Thomas Hughes was for sale. The farm's strong appeal was its orchards and the large thatched roof farmhouse, which could adequately accommodate her entire family. All its furniture was included in the sale of the farmhouse. The bakery was sold and the farm purchased around 1887. To complete her plans, Catherine set about arranging the marriage of her eldest son, Michael, to Bridget Walsh of Rathgranaher. They were married about 1890. Michael was twenty-eight and Bridget eighteen. Their first daughter, Katie was born in 1892. Tim, Nora, my mother, William, PJ, and Edward followed. All were born within nine years.

The marriage grew to be an unhappy union between two incompatible individuals. Michael was unsuited for farming. He disliked hard work and the long hours. A philosophical conversation at the local pub with his colleagues, along with a friendly drink, suited him better. His time spent away from the farm and neglecting his chores caused friction with his family. Bridget was equally unaccustomed to the rigors of housework and raising a large family. Like her mother, she was a skillful dressmaker and loved needlework. Bridget became affected by the isolation and neglect. By now she too, had found solace in the bottle. Matters would have been worse were it not for Catherine, her mother-in-law, who lived with them. Her guidance kept affairs in some order. Catherine's business skills ensured that the salable produces of the orchard and garden reached the market in Ballinrobe. The Bunnadubber farm's legendary orchards continued to produce an income until 1960.

There was little sorrow or regret when Michael announced his intention to go to America. Without waiting for the birth of his son, Edward, he set sail in 1901, leaving his entire family behind. He found a job as a timekeeper for Cleveland Cliffs, an iron ore shipper that sailed the Great Lakes. Unlike many of his countrymen, he did not make his fortune in America. He sent home money on rare occasions. He grew content among his newly found friends and the clerical work was not very demanding.

Meanwhile, back in Ireland, Catherine was holding the family together. "I was raised by my grandmother Catherine," Nora, my mother, explained. "Bridget, my mother, could not handle the responsibility of a family. She often sat in the corner of a room, staring into space, unaware of what was going on around her," Nora told me. "My mother was melancholy."

Later in life, I understood this to be depression when the same thing happened to members of my own family.

In my mother's grade school, the children were taught Gaelic, which was an innovation. The English, who had controlled the land for hundreds of years, did not allow the Irish to speak Gaelic. "I found it too difficult to learn," Mother said. "My teacher let me slide along if I helped him handle the younger students. All the children were in one room at our schoolhouse."

Nora loved life in Ireland. They lived in a large house with an even bigger barn, which also served as a kitchen. "The barn was large enough for the Irish Republican Army (IRA) to drill there and they did," she said. "It had a dirt floor, which made it a great place to hold a dance. On Friday nights, my sister, Katie, and I would go down to the country lane to meet the fellows."

"Do not bring any of those boys here to dance," her Grandmother instructed. These words usually fell on deaf ears, as Nora loved to dance.

One family member of the Haire family after another joined their father in Cleveland, Ohio. There were no jobs for them in Ireland so most of the eligible men immigrated either to England or America. The Haire girls followed their brothers, except for PJ, who remained behind to run the family farm.

"I hated to leave," Nora said, "but my grandmother insisted that I go, too." Nora traveled on *The Lapland Steam Ship* landing at Ellis Island, the immigration port of entry to America on June 1, 1915. She was nineteen at the time. Due to ignorance, the authorities added an "O" to her name. Mother always claimed, "The O'Haires she knew in Ireland were hillbillies."

Nora's first job in America was as an upstairs maid for a wealthy family living in Bratenahl, Ohio. "That's where the swells of the day lived in fine style," she told me. She lived on the third floor of the mansion with all the other help. This was a normal starting position for an Irish lassie. She lived the life of a servant; making the beds, cleaning and dusting, washing clothes and polishing the fine silverware used by the people that employed her. She enjoyed her routine and made instant friends with the other household help.

The Irish Club took care of her other social needs, like meeting men. Cleveland had a bar owned by the Irish where the immigrants could meet their fellow countrymen. Drinking, dancing and eating were the main draw, but if you needed a job that was also the place to go to find one. Just announce that you were looking for a job and before the evening was over somebody would approach you with an offer. That is how Mother found a position in a factory. It was piecework where the more pieces you could produce the more money you could earn. She became incredibly efficient and was such a novelty that her boss liked to show her off. The fact that she was an auburn haired beauty may have added to her mystique. Her good income now gave her considerable freedom.

One of the men she met, but not at the Irish Club, was Leslie Kelly. A near teetotaler, he considered himself thoroughly English and thought the Irish frivolous, so he did not hang around at the Irish Club. Nora's father introduced them. He saw Leslie as a well-dressed, prosperous man with a good job at The White Motor Company. Leslie's job required traveling, which allowed Nora to have other suitors. One of these suitors was an Irish attorney.

Nora favored the attorney and planned to meet him at the big Saturday night dance. "I was not going to be distracted by Leslie, as he was out of town delivering one of his fire engines," she told me. "At the proper moment when I was going to make my move, in walked Leslie dressed in a royal blue blazer with white duck trousers. I was smitten! If he hadn't arrived at just that moment, your father might have been an attorney."

Nora O'Haire and Leslie Kelly were married in 1920. George was born in 1921 and Rita in 1923. Life was moving too fast for her. The prospect of getting pregnant again was more than she could handle. It was time for Nora to get away. She understood her mother's plight better now. Catherine, her grandmother, died in 1919 at the age of seventy-eight. After about four years of living with only PJ's to help her, Nora felt that her mother now needed her. Nora took her two children and sailed for Ireland. She thoroughly enjoyed herself there.

"A man with a motorcar parked in front of our house every morning just hoping the rich American woman would request his services," she told me. "He acted as a guide taking me to places I had never been before. I was happy in Ireland and hated the idea of leaving my mother. It was only after your father threatened to cut off my supply of money that I returned to America. We had been in Ireland for eleven months. By the time we returned home, little George spoke English with an Irish brogue."

Back in the States, Nora's life began to resemble her mother's. Children came tumbling forth regularly. Over the next ten years she gave birth to Betty, Frank, John, Mark and Kevin. With the accident in 1933, Leslie's fortune evaporated. Nora was never the same. She seemed overwhelmed by her circumstances. Mother, like Dad, had grown comfortable during the good times. Now she was living like the poor folks she knew so well back in Ireland. Her religion was all that held her together. Mother saw the Church as her refuge.

"You give all my money to the Church," Dad said. Mother did give her money away, but not always to the Church. No panhandler ever walked away from our back door without something to eat. If they asked for money and she had any, they got it. This frustrated my father even more. He had no faith in God, only in himself.

"Actually, you can't give money away," Mother told me. "If you give it to a good cause it will come back a hundred-fold." On the way to daily Mass, a forlorn looking man stopped us and asked Mother for help. Willingly she gave him her last dollar. She had been planning to buy milk and bread on our way back from church. Now she did not have any money for our food. When we got home, there was another man waiting for us.

"Here is the five dollars I owe you," he told her.

"I'm sorry, but I don't remember loaning you any money," Mother said to him.

"That doesn't matter," he insisted, handing it to her. She gladly took the money and sent me back to the store to get the groceries we needed.

This presented a problem for the store owner and me. I had a speech impediment. Only people used to my speech pattern could understand what I was saying. The family called it "baby talk." With the other children in school and Kevin being a baby, I was the only one Mother could send to the store. She gave me a note in her very best handwriting, but only a fellow Irishman could read her writing. I rarely came home with the right items.

Mother lived a good, saintly, existence, but those living with a Holy One do not always appreciate the Saint in their midst. Mother's choices were difficult to understand at times. She, like Dad, was a mystery to me and to others in our family.

Sister's Gift To The Bishop

Every morning Mother took me and Kevin, my brother, to Mass at Immaculate Conception Catholic Church. We were the youngest of the seven children. Our siblings were all in school at that hour. The church had beautiful stained glass windows. They were renowned, having been imported from Italy in the late 1800's. I loved that church.

On the way to church, we passed an elementary school. At that time of morning, the school children would be running and playing. Sounds of laughter and joy came from all directions. I could hardly wait to be old enough to go to kindergarten.

When the day came for me to enter school, I said goodbye to Mother and Kevin and gladly joined the children playing in the schoolyard. What I did not realize was that there was more to school than playing. Kindergarten only lasted half a day. Why did they expect us to take a nap?

In the class was a blonde, silky-haired girl, with large soft brown eyes. Her name was Mary Lou. Her hair was always pulled back by a pretty bow. I am sure I never mentioned how much I liked her. She took quite a shine to me, and the feeling was mutual. One day she planted a big kiss on my cheek. I was smitten!

For the first grade, I left public school and went to a parochial school. The New school belonged to the parish with the lovely church. Mary Lou was in my class. I loved first grade, I was the teacher's pet. The second grade was better yet. Sister Mary Dolors adored me, and I her.

Sister Mary Dolors told me that I was going to play the Christ Child in a pageant. The Bishop of Cleveland would be there with his assistants. We practiced my walk down the aisle. It had to be very slow. Even my hand had to be held in such a way as to make it look as though I were blessing the Bishop and his friends. This was very important to Sister. She explained that I had been chosen from all the schoolchildren of the Diocese. Sister Mary Dolors probably had a lot to do with that! True, people did say that I looked like an angel. My hair was a mass of blonde curls. I was shown a picture of the Christ Child. There were the curls, just like mine.

The reason my hair was a mass of curls was because we were poor and could not afford to get haircuts. With seven children, haircuts were not a high priority. Clothes were passed down from brother to brother and sister to sister. Being the fourth of five brothers, they were usually not in great shape by the time they reached me. However, for this special occasion Mother decided that I should have new clothes and a haircut!

When I arrived at the appointed time for the pageant, Sister was horrified! "What happened to your beautiful curls?" she cried before she could stop herself. I had been happy about my haircut because my Mother was so proud of it. When tears formed in Sister's eyes I knew instantly it had been a big mistake. She wrapped her arms around me and brought me into the folds of her habit, trying to keep me from seeing her disappointment. She held me for quite a while, until she could stop crying, and come up with a new plan. My hair was not as short as she had first thought. In fact, it was long enough to make new curls with a hot curling iron. Before long I looked like my old self and the *curly perm* for men had just been invented!

In a room off the lobby of St. John's Cathedral, Sister Mary Dolors removed my clothes. I remember standing in my underwear, brand-new, thank God! She put me into a floor-length white gown. To add to the effect, she had made a halo out of silver poster board, which was taped to my head. Now I looked just like the picture of the Christ Child she had shown me.

To the sounds of an organ playing some grand processional hymn, they stationed me at the doors of the cathedral. A nun on either side opened the doors. My eyes widened. There was a sea of black and white. It looked like a church full of penguins. Nuns had come from all parts of the city. They were all turned towards me as if they were expecting the Lord himself. More importantly, there was the Bishop! A white cloth runner on the floor led straight to him. The organ music swelled as Sister gave me the signal to start up the aisle. They expected me to pull a sled loaded with gifts for the Bishop and his assistants. As I tried to take a step forward the sled would not budge. The friction between it and the white runner glued the sled in its place. Leaning forward with all my weight, I pulled on the rope. The sled broke free. I almost fell on my face, not very dignified for the Christ Child. I could hear a gasp from one of the nuns. Quickly regaining my composure, I tried again. The next step was as hard as the first. Keeping the sled moving was difficult enough—never mind the slow pace! There was little chance that I could keep in time with the lovely music. Finally,

I got the correct lean to my body. I did not want to disappoint Sister any further.

After a very long walk, with the Bishop watching every step of the way; I finally reached him. It was probably his prayers and those of Sister Mary Dolors that got me to the front of the cathedral. I bestowed my blessing and turned to the gifts. The first was a lovely box wrapped in colored foil and decorated with a flower that resembled a porcupine. It was made from striped colored drinking straws. I have yet to see a more impressive wrapping job. As I tried to lift the box, it nearly slipped through my hands. It weighed a ton or more!

After each of the assistants received my blessing and their equally weighty gift, we broke for refreshments. In the reception hall with the Bishop and his assistants standing around talking, I received hugs from most of the nuns present. Sister Mary Dolors did not look anything like her name (Dolors meaning sadness). She beamed with happiness, as proud as any mother! Apparently, her gift to the Bishop was me!

54.
The Measure of a Man
Sara Burnside

One was born into a typical American family, the other born into an atypical family; one of wealth, the other of poverty. One's father was known, the other's not. One aspired to replicate his father's journey, the other to rise above his father's example. One attended a private school, the other public. Both attended Eastern colleges. Both men worked hard to succeed; one in business, the other in community action. One had enough wealth to bank overseas, the other struggled to pay off college loans. Both men married intelligent, accomplished women and raised beautiful children.

Both were determined to become president of the United States and were nominated by their respective political parties. One failed in his goal, the other is now serving his second term as President of our country.

The measure of a man matters. Who he is, his character, shines through everything he does. People see his actions, his essence, and judge accordingly. Each of us, as voters in a free country, decided. I think the better man won.

NOTE: I am unapologetic Democrat. So it is not surprising that I would find Barack Obama the better man to be President of our country.

55.
The Midnight Ride of Who?
Al Rosie

Prologue

Listen, my children and I'll unveil
The facts behind a fanciful tale
For over a century spun to our youth
From a poet who couldn't quite handle the truth
The smith, Paul Revere worked in silver and copper
Concerning his ride there's an infamous whopper
Concocted by Longfellow, famed in his time
For Hi'watha, The Blacksmith and works deemed sublime
Poor Longfellow lacked a good rhyme dictionary
And so was compelled to be quite fictionary
When stumped for a rhyme for hear and for year
He eventually settled on good Paul Revere
With the proper resource he'd have penned that the cause
Was better abetted by bold William Dawes
Who completed his ride while Revere was thwarted
When captured by Redcoats his ride was aborted.
So always remember when musing with Clio[1]
Some authors may tend to jazz up a bio
Don't believe every book on the library shelf.
Some folks bend the truth Not excluding myself [2]

1: Clio was the Greek muse of history.

2: Dawes was apprehended with Revere at Lexington but escaped. Samuel Prescott was the only one to reach concord, but the only rhyme I could think of was "hot to trot".

56.
The Need for Sane Gun Control Laws
Sara Burnside

The 2nd Amendment: A well-regulated Militia, being necessary to the security of a free State, the right of the people to keep and bear Arms, shall not be infringed.

First, let's make clear that many of our Amendments were added as our country determined it necessary as our democracy evolved. So to say that our forefathers were absolutely wise in all considerations; is untrue. For example, the 18th, which prohibited alcohol, was later determined unwise in the 21st Amendment. We learn as a nation, as we go along. My reading of the 2nd Amendment is that at the time, our society was more like the wild west, without the protection of a trained police force. Also uppermost in their minds was the concern that a Presidency would become a Monarchy, thus the need for a State Militia.

Those that would oppose any gun regulation may have ulterior motives that have nothing to do with the welfare of our people. This was so when slavery was considered civil more due to the commercial needs of the South rather than what was moral. Of course, there are those that enjoy the sport of shooting, even perhaps with automatic weapons. One does have to have a license to hunt which doesn't seem to offend the NRA. And for the later, why not have regulated shooting ranges. Individual ownership of any available weapons is simply not necessary in a civilized society. Research has shown that when people have their own guns they are often shot with them by criminal intruders. To suggest that teachers be armed and trained to protect themselves and children is not practical. Even police officers and military members report that even as trained and experienced shooters, they sometimes do not hit their mark. For a nation that has more per-capita guns than Yemen, let's allow sane and practical gun control laws. Our innocent children and victims demand it now.

NOTE: As a non-gun-enthusiast, I still don't understand why this issue is so controversial.

57.
The Promise
Alice Lezotte

Dawn's glorious radiance, pink golden light,
Sparkling dewdrop kisses, a magical sight,

Birds' joyous songs lacing blue skies,
Bubbles of children's laughter gaily arise,

"Good morning" greetings start the day.
New hopes and beginnings, new adventures

     Hooray!

58.
The Skunk
Al Rosie

Methinks

She stinks.

59.
The User Used
Diana Kathryn Plopa

Once in quiet solitude
I walked a distant shore
I watched the waves roll in
And subside as in ancient lore
The wonder and the beauty
Took me by surprise
The perfection in its simplicity
The crest of a moonlit tide
Now I walk in a solitude
Interrupted by deafening noise
Screams of fear interjected
With cries of breaking toys
All around me dwells a pressure
Simple existence – s struggle – a fight
I scream as protecting darkness
Gives birth to horror with awakening light
Silently I sit here screaming
With these thoughts that I whore
I yearn for that quiet solitude
For calm to return once more

60.
The Zug Island Anthem
Al Rosie

*Zug Island was a peninsula located at the confluence of the Detroit
and Rouge Rivers until a shipping canal was constructed through it
in the late nineteenth century. Currently houses the US Steel facility
but is also home to wildlife such as peregrine falcons and foxes.
Neighbors don't appreciate noise and aroma wafting from the site
and Canadians have complained about earthquake like tremors
seventy miles away.*

Though I've travelled round the globe a dozen times
And been everywhere from Rangipur to Rome
Though I've traversed all the continents and climes
There is no place like the showplace I call home.

It's Zug Island, Beautiful Zug Island
Flower of the rivers in full bloom
Zug Island, Beautiful Zug Island
Makes the Taj Mahal look like a tomb.

Though I've from Brigadoon to Timbuktu
Seen the pyramids and even Shangri La
In my travelogue I must confide to you
My exotic spot makes all the rest seem blah.

Zug Island, Beautiful Zug Island
See it loom majestic through the fumes
Zug Island, Beautiful Zug Island
Never have you smelled such sweet perfumes.

I've been bored in Bora Bora and Tahiti
And the sights of Bali simply make me shrug
The Wall of China's covered with graffiti
They cannot compete with my sweet Isle of Zug.

Zug Island, Beautiful Zug Island
Paradise of the planet, I disclose
Zug Island, Beautiful Zug Island
You can find it just by following your nose.

61.
This Here... Place
B. Silver

This here's a story about a cabbage... and about how he spent his early days livin' and laughin' in the patch. He was a small patch cabbage who liked nothing more than sittin' in the sun, kickin' the dirt around with his roots.

Being that this patch where he lived was small and away from all the noise and congestion of those great metropolis patches, he took pride in knowin' most of the others who lived nearby. Even for its small size, this patch had quite the heterogeneous population.

Why, there was the Spanish onion across the patch at the outskirts. The Carrot bunch over in the next furrow. The Black-eyed peas just this side of the waterline. Them Broccoli's, a nice bunch, ya know, they's from good stock. And on the east side were the Tulips who, incidentally, had just come back from winter vacation. Heard tell they was all the way gone to China.

"Hogwash, I say," said the cabbage one day.

Funny thing one day last spring.... the cabbage threatened to roll over and crush the carrot if'n she didn't stop leanin' over on him and blockin' out the sun. Really wasn't nothing, though. Cabbage like to throw their weight around because they think they're so big and tough-leaved. But, over and about, it's really a nice, quiet community. Clean, too!

Water department sees to it everyone's property is kept moist with the new spigots they put in.

Near every day someone is always coming 'round to clean up the furrows and keep the grass out. That grass, you know, they can be a nuisance if they ain't taken care of proper. Why, they just move in quick as ladybugs and poke their pointy noses inside everybody's business. They get under roots and even push some of them others out.

Shame the way some plants act. But them folks comin' round every day, they take right fast care of 'em. Yes sir, them scrawny little things... they ain't gonna mess around where they ain't wanted.

Lookin' around and about, though, don't think you could find a nicer bunch of vegetables.

That cabbage is gone, now. Yeah, he moved out late last harvest. His son lives there, now. Looks just like his dad, too.

Yeah, guess they just keep on comin' until one day the land goes bad or whatever.

Heard tell yesterday if the land quits they might just plow it under and try and get the fruits to move in. Boy, that would be somethin', wouldn't it.

WSU 1972

62.
Tick Tock, Tick Tock
Renee Batenjany

Tick Tack, Tick Tock, what is this racing up, down and all around!

Tick Tack, Tick Tack, why can't this crazy fast pace stop!

Tick Tack, Tick Tock, why must we keep a stepping pace with it all!

Tick Tock, Tick Tock, it is here now!

Tick Tock, Tick Tock, it has left us a story of our past!

Tick -rock, Tick Tock, it will indeed set the future for all!

Tick Tock, Tick Tock, do you feel it now!

Tick Tock, Tick Tock, Time it will forever live on!

63.
To Our Wives
Jerry McKeon

You are my Garden of Eden
Growing wildly in my heart
Sowing seeds of contentment
A fruitful bounty you impart

You are the sunshine at dawn
Helping make my garden grow
You are the warm spring rains
Bringing fertility to my soul

You are the bees that pollinate
Leaving new life on every vine
You are earthworms in the soil
Leaving a tilled earth behind

You're the juicy rich fruit
That I passionately devour
You're the fragrance of the garden
From the abundance of flowers

This garden of life is eternal
Living forever in my heart
It will continue to sow its blessings
Long after death tears us apart

64.
Toast
Celia P. Ransom

If you asked what I like to eat the most,
My response would undoubtedly be wheat toast.
With coffee each morn I consume slices three
It starts my day off just as I want it to be.

And should I perchance miss this first meal
Everything in my day unwinds like a reel.
Not a breakfast of champions I'm sure you'd agree
But 'tis the one that works the very best for me.

65.
Trillium
Celia P. Ransom

Splashes of white along the roadside,
Delicate petals by woods edge abide.
Casting off winter, having survived,
Proclaiming once more, spring has arrived.

66.
Turtle Tales
Jerry McKeon

Authors are just like turtles in their shells
All circled around a table with stories to tell
Their races left unguarded for everyone to see
But their life under the shell remains a mystery

Their lives are hidden like a clandestine spy
To get information you need a private eye
They all have stories they would love to sell
So many stories but not their own pray tell

Some teachers, a lawyer, and industry chiefs
Their past not their readings are always brief
Poems and stories are members claim to fame
But no one at the table has fame to claim

There's humor and sadness in stones they pen
Sometimes messages in written word they send
Everyone at the table reads for a critique
But a bit about their past is hardly every leaked

Recently a biography on each was submitted
That's a lot more than they ever contributed
The turtles are now coming out of their shell
And now everyone has another story to tell

67.
Uncle Sam's Yacht
Mark A. Kelly

The Helmsman

Before I turned twenty-one, I traveled around the world on my uncle's yacht – Uncle Sam that is! I was in the Navy. The yacht was the J W Weeks DD 701, a destroyer.

One of the many great adventures began on a cold, windy evening as our ship plowed through the Pacific Ocean. The spray from the waves, breaking over the flying bridge, soaked me to the skin. I was freezing. This started me thinking. *It was time I devised a scheme to get off this lookout watch.* When relieved for the night, I went to take a shower. Looking into the mirror I saw crystals of salt glistening in the light. My face was covered from the spray. After a shower, I lay in my rack working on a plan. The next thing I knew, the PA was waking the sailors for yet another day. Sleep had not solved my dilemma. *Standing yet another watch will be a better time and place to develop my plan,* I thought.

Part of the Navy's great system was to fully utilize every man aboard ship by assigning each of them many duties. The two main jobs were sailing and fighting. To keep the ship moving under normal or non-combat conditions, each person had to participate by manning an underway watch. These watches were considered sailing duties.

During normal steaming, only a sixth of the crew was required to man the ship at one time. This meant most people had to stand watch some for a four-hour sea watch every twenty hours. During daylight hours, anyone not on watch was supposed to be honing his fighting skills. This usually meant working on our equipment to keep it in top fighting condition. This kept everyone fully committed, but not necessarily interested. It was a busy life. If one did get bored, it was usually while standing some mindless underway watch.

While at sea, the bridge is the highest point above the waterline manned on a continuous basis. That is where the Captain stations himself to control the ship. The wheelhouse is the enclosure on the bridge where most of the instruments are located. The flying bridge is an open walkway that surrounds the wheelhouse. Many men are required to operate the bridge. It can be an exciting place. However standing the port side lookout watch, on the flying bridge; was not one of them. That was my watch station.

It was a watchman's job to discover anything out of the ordinary in that vast Pacific Ocean, like a ship or an airplane. Spotting something was exciting but seldom did anything appear. During the daylight, I found the sea to be interesting. The least little change signified something. A break in the pattern was worth investigating. Sometimes it would be caused by a flying fish, a dolphin or a shark. On rare occasions, it would be some debris, but it could be a submarine periscope.

There were three other destroyers in our squadron traveling with us. If one of them happened to be running abreast, I studied its every detail.

The sky was of less interest, as there were no birds or airplanes out at sea. But I kept looking just in case. At night, it was the opposite. There were millions of stars. I tried to learn and identify the various constellations. Otherwise, four hours of nothing to report could get pretty boring, especially on a night when I was sleepy!

While gazing out to sea a few nights later, I sighted a ship off in the distance. "Ahoy. Ship off the port bow," I reported loud and clear.

"Which way is it heading?" Lieutenant Hermann, the OOD (Officer of the Deck), asked. He was the acting Captain for the night watch on the bridge.

"I can't tell, Sir," I answered.

"What'd you mean, Sailor?" came his incredulous voice. "Don't you know the rules of the road?"

"Yes, Sir," I snapped, knowing he meant which running light was I observing on the other ship, red port, green starboard. If I knew the color of the light, I certainly knew which direction the ship was heading. "I can't tell, Sir. I'm colorblind." I could indeed tell red from green running lights, but this was my plan to get off this watch. The OOD was at my side in a heartbeat asking me to point out the intruding ship. As acting Captain, he had to know everything that was going on during his watch.

"The light is red," he observed out loud. "So which way is the ship heading?"

"It is heading east, most likely back to the States, Sir," I answered.

"So you know which way we are heading," he said, half to himself.

"West," I said. He seemed impressed that I knew which way we were heading.

"How is it that you're in the Navy if you are colorblind?" Lieutenant Hermann asked.

"They must need men."

"I thought being colorblind would disqualify you from serving in the Navy," he observed.

"It disqualified me from attending the Fire Control School. That's why they shipped me back from DC, Sir."

"Yes, I heard you washed out of school, but nobody said why." I told him the whole story, partly to keep him talking. It relieved the boredom. He listened and even seemed sympathetic. I liked Lieutenant Hermann and considered him the best of all the officers. He was always pleasant with the ordinary seamen, even though he looked as rough as a fullback for the Annapolis Football team.

The next time I came to the bridge the Quartermaster stopped me. "Your new watch station is the bridge messenger."

"Who's going to take over the port side watch?" I asked.

"The old bridge messenger," came the reply.

I thought being the messenger was a step up. Now I'd be able to run around the ship carrying messages for the OOD. *That should be much more interesting than staring at an empty sea.*

Wrong. I spent very little time off the bridge. Instead, I had to stand next to the OOD most of the time being constantly alert. There was even less to keep me occupied than standing the port side lookout. *Had my plan backfired?* At least the wheelhouse was far more tolerable in foul weather than standing out in the open. There, I would be a target for all the elements the sea chose to throw at me.

Before long, I understood how things worked on the bridge. So little happened under normal steaming conditions I soon felt I could take over for the Captain. The busiest sailor on the bridge was the helmsman. He was constantly spinning the wheel that steers the ship, even though we may not change course during the entire four-hour watch. Once when the OOD stepped out of the wheelhouse I asked the helmsman, "Why do you keep spinning the wheel?"

"If I don't, the waves will push the ship off course in a matter of minutes," he answered.

"How do you know which way to turn?" I asked.

"Stand on the balls of your feet. Do you feel the ship moving?"

"Yes."

"Notice how you can feel the stern of the ship start to rise?" he asked.

"Yes," I answered again.

"If you feel it in your right foot then you spin the wheel to the starboard," he instructed. "Then wait for the stern to rise in your left foot. That's when you spin the wheel to port."

I watched him as I stood there. Sure enough, I could feel it! I pretended to be handling the wheel, to see if I would turn it, at the same time and in the same direction as the helmsman. Then I tried to see if I could sense the new direction before the helmsman did. It was easy to learn how to steer the ship the way he explained it.

"Can I try it?" I asked the helmsman.

"If the OOD says it's okay," the helmsman answered.

Lieutenant Hermann happened to be on watch that night. "Sure," he said, agreeing to let me try.

I caught on immediately, thanks to the helmsman's clear instructions. Everyone seemed pleased at my success. *Just a new game to break the monotony,* I thought.

Crossing the Date Line meant we lost a day in our lives. As we passed over the line, the calendar went from November 29 to December 1. Somehow we passed through time completely skipping November 30. It was as if we were space travelers in a science fiction movie.

The person most directly affected by the *lost day* was Cecil Hesslen, a rather quiet gentleman in Fire Control. His birthday was November 30. His claim to fame was that he got his birthday back one hour at a time as we passed through the different time zones around the world. In the middle of the night, there was one watch that only lasted two hours. The Navy changes their clocks during that short watch, extending it to three hours. Cecil was usually on watch at that time. Thus, he got part of his birthday back by standing an extra hour on watch.

About a thousand miles from Japan we were smacked by a typhoon. A typhoon is the Pacific's equivalent of an Atlantic hurricane. During the three or four days of this typhoon, a third of the ship's crew became seasick. Even the Junior OOD was throwing up in a pail on the bridge.

Those that did not get sick were said to have gotten their *sea legs*. Those with sea legs were required to stand watch every four hours instead of every eight. The ship needed all the help she could get in the rough seas. The Navy made me a permanent helmsman at this time.

Steering a Naval Destroyer through that typhoon was exhilarating! I had to continually spin the wheel, first to the starboard than to the port. The bow was either plunging into a giant wave that washed completely over the wheelhouse, or the ship was so far out of the water I thought we were flying. Even in the daylight we could not see our sister ships most of the time. If we were in a trough; all we could see around us was a wall of water. If we were riding the crest of a wave; the other ships were usually in a trough and out of sight.

"Kelly, you're doing a fine job at the helm," Lieutenant Hermann, the OOD, said.

"How does he know?" I asked the duty Quartermaster. The OOD seldom looked at the compass.

"Just watch the ship's wake the next time you are on the flying bridge or the fantail (the back of the ship). Even in rough seas the ship leaves a very distinct trail called a wake. If the helmsman is minding the wheel, the wake will be straight as an arrow. This is one of the ways the OOD keeps an eye on his helmsman."

Another benefit of the typhoon was no waiting in the chow line. With only two-thirds of the crew eating and half of them standing watch; there was no line. Plenty of room to sit at the tables and nobody was harassing me.

While I was learning to steer the ship we sailed across the International Date Line located between Midway Island and Japan. The Navy made a big deal about the crossing. All sailors aboard ship that were crossing the International Date Line for the first time were inducted into the Realm of the Golden Dragon with the words,

Know ye, that Mark A Kelly on the 29th day of November, 1953 aboard the John W Weeks at Latitude 28 degrees, 15 minutes North, Longitude 180 degrees East, appeared on the Threshold of the Far East, and having been duly inspected and found worthy, was accepted into the Ancient and Sacred Order of the Golden Dragon.

The only privilege accorded a member of the *Ancient Order of the Golden Dragon* seemed to be the fact that we could legally wear dragons sewn on the inside cuffs of our blouse. It was common for sailors to do that, but not legal. I now understood why they wanted those dragons - it made them feel like *Old Salts*. For me, it was now legal, but I never bothered to do it.

About a thousand miles from Japan we were smacked by a typhoon. A typhoon is the Pacific's equivalent of an Atlantic hurricane. During the three or four days of this typhoon, a third of the ship's crew became seasick. Even the Junior OOD was throwing up in a pail on the bridge.

Those that did not get sick were said to have gotten their *sea legs*. Those with sea legs were required to stand watch every four hours instead of every eight. The ship needed all the help she could get in the rough seas. The Navy made me a permanent helmsman at this time.

Japan December 1953

As the *John W Weeks* came out of the typhoon, we spotted the coastline of Japan. Our ship headed directly for the once proud Imperial Japanese Naval Base at Yokosuka. This was during the Korean War and Japan was still very much under the influence of the American Occupation. We maneuvered into our designated slip and tied up alongside one of our sister ships at the dock. It was December 9, 1953, two days after the anniversary of Pearl Harbor Day. The significance of that event was lost on us in the excitement. We were to see our first truly foreign country with all its unfamiliar customs and language.

After we tied up at the dock, shore leave was announced. "Liberty starts with the starboard side watch crew." *That's me!* I was among the first of our crew to set foot on Japanese soil. As the happy sailors headed off to the nearest bar, I went on a mission of my own—to find my brother, John. For the last year and a half, he had been stationed at Haneda Air Force Base near Tokyo, Japan.

Not realizing things were probably quite different in a foreign land; I headed off in search of a public telephone booth, not even considering they may not have such a thing in Japan. The

Naval base actually had a public telephone booth. I picked up the receiver.

"May I help you?" a sweet young voice said in perfect English. I was astounded.

"Give me Haneda Air Force Base, please." It never occurred to me that I didn't have any Japanese money nor did I speak the language. The next thing I knew she switched me to a long distance operator.

"May I help you?" a second sweet voice said. She too spoke perfect English with only a slight Oriental accent.

"May I speak to John Kelly at Haneda Air Force Base?" I repeated my request, without considering the operator at Haneda might not even know John Kelly.

"May I help you?" John's voice answered. How incredible! He was on duty that night and answered the telephone himself.

"This is your brother, Mark."

"Yes, I recognized your voice, but I can't believe it!" he explained. John had no idea where I was since I stopped my letter writing before we left the States. How could he be talking to his younger brother on the telephone here in Japan?

"Where are you?" he asked. Quickly I explained my situation. "Can you come to Tokyo this weekend?" John asked.

"I don't know. We normally can't get overnight liberty in a foreign port. How far is Haneda from Yokosuka?"

"A couple of hours south of here," he answered, not thinking anything was unusual in his request.

"How do I get there?" I asked.

"Just hop the train," he said. *Had he ever been to Yokosuka, I wondered, but did not think to ask.* I was too excited about the possibility of seeing him to worry about such details. *We Kellys were more than willing to take adventuresome trips without thinking of the consequences.*

"Where do I get my money exchanged to Japanese currency?" I asked him.

"You can use American Scrip most places in Japan."

I already had some Scrip because that is what the Navy used to pay us upon reaching Japan. "I'll go back to my ship and see about a weekend pass," I told John. He gave me instructions as to how to get to Tokyo by train and then by bus to his base.

I hung up the phone and was out of the booth on my way back to the ship before realizing the remarkable thing that just happened! I made a phone call in a foreign land, without any phone number or coin of the realm, nor could I speak a word of the native tongue. Such is the naiveté of youth!

When I got back to our ship, I explained to my boss Seidel that I wanted to go to Tokyo to see my brother.

"Can I get a weekend pass?" I asked him.

"I don't know. Let's try and see."

First he took the request for a weekend pass to the Chief. The Chief okayed it. Next he went to the duty officer. Fortunately for me, it was my friend, Lieutenant Hermann. He signed the pass and took it to the Executive Officer himself. The Exec, also named Kelly, who was acting Captain, liked the idea and authorized my pass. They were oblivious to the difficulties that could arise. Apparently, they were all wrapped up in the excitement of my getting a chance to visit my brother. They did not seem concerned that I, a twenty--year-old, was about to trek across the land of our enemies of just a few years ago. We Americans had bombed their buildings and destroyed their way of life. And we still occupied their country. The Japanese must hate all Americans, especially servicemen. Now I was daring to travel alone, without benefit of a guide, not to mention the fact I did not know where I was going, and might lose my way and never return.

If I spent any time thinking about these facts, I probably would have just headed for the nearest bar along with the other sailors. Instead, I continued in this naïve fashion all the time I was in Japan, or I probably never would have gotten out of the Yokosuka Naval Base.

Finding my way proved easy as most of the directional signs were written in three languages. The top was written in what I think was Chinese. The middle I assumed to be Japanese and the bottom was, thank God, English. They directed me to the train station. The express train I caught, bound for Tokyo, was incredibly modern and extremely fast. The trip only took an hour and a half. The only stop I remembered it making was Yokohama.

From the train station in Tokyo, I had little difficulty finding the bus to the air base. I just followed the signs, as John had described them. The bus displayed a sign "Airport." I arrived safely at the Tokyo International Airport terminal, which was also the Haneda Air Force Base. The American Armed Forces were running the airport. John told me to look for him behind the airline ticket counter.

There he was! We just stood looking at each other. It was almost two years since we were last together. He was in his Airman uniform, I in my Navy one. He looked no different to me. I had seen him in uniform before. John had never seen me in mine. I must have looked quite different. His little brother had grown up. We hugged, not an abnormal occurrence at any terminal, but an airman and a sailor? We both started talking at once. So much to say! We finally settled behind the ticket counter where John worked. It was time to catch up on recent happenings.

"Dick Cavanaugh was just in from Korea for R&R rest and recreation)," John told me. Dick was a high school buddy of ours and one of *The Barons*. "He stopped by to see me and showed me pictures of himself with Debbie Reynolds. She and Dick were standing by the airplane that brought her to Korea."

"She's one of my favorite movie stars," I told John.

"She was there to entertain the troops," John explained. "Dick also had pictures of Keenan Wynn and Walter Pigeon." They were popular male movie stars of the day. Dick later sent copies of those pictures to me; he was mighty proud of them.

At one point, while John and I were leaning on the ticket counter talking, John said, "Excuse me," as he reached across for something on my side of the counter. I didn't pay any attention to what he was doing, just got out of his way. A singsong voice speaking in Japanese came over the PA announcing the arrival of a flight from America, Hawaii and cities in that direction. The only words I understood were the names of the different cities.

"How was that?" John asked me.

"How was what?"

"The announcement?"

"How do I know? I don't understand Japanese."

"No, the fact that I made that announcement."

"You did not!" I said, since to me the voice was obviously Japanese and did not sound anything like my brother.

"Watch this!" he said, as he picked up a microphone and began the announcement over again. It was indeed John, speaking to the world in Japanese. We were definitely in another world that day!

The Baron Of Tokyo December 1953

While John and I stood behind the ticket counter of the Tokyo International Airport, my brother explained his work duties.

"Being in the Air Force is more like working a civilian job. My shift lasts eight hours and then I'm off for the rest of the day unless I am on flying status."

"It's not like that in the Navy," I said. "We usually stand a four-hour watch every twelve hours and then return to our regular job. It keeps us mighty busy, especially while at sea."

After John's shift ended, we went back to his barracks to sleep. When we got up, it was late in the afternoon.

"Are you ready for some excitement?" John asked. "Why don't we head into Tokyo?" He didn't wait for an answer. "I wish I had some civvies that would fit you," John observed. "You've gotten taller and heavier than me. Speaking of clothes, I was just at the tailor's picking up this suit. The lady working at the *New Fox Tailor Shop* said that she sees me at the *Blue Chateau* all the time."

"Toxan cool," she said.

"That means she thinks I'm a cool number," John explained. "*Blue Chateau* is a great place to hear music. I go there all the time."

We headed into Tokyo. John wore his tailor-made clothes, a dark blue civilian suit, white shirt, dark tie and blue suede shoes. I wore my Navy blue dress uniform. I'd learned a lot about his tour of duty in Japan by this time, but still did not know what to expect.

"I have a routine I follow when in Tokyo," John explained. "First I go to the FEAF Club (Far East Air Force Enlisted Man's Club) for a drink. It's located across the street from the Imperial Palace where the Emperor lives."

"Have you ever seen him?"

"No. I never see anybody over there. It is very serene."

John went back to his description of his routine. "If I have a date with Yoshiko, she meets me there. I wish you could see her. She's delightful and very attractive. Yoshiko is an overseas telephone operator and speaks perfect English. We first met on the phone when she called the base on official business. I tried to get her to meet with me, but she didn't want to date an American. It took a lot of persuasion on my part before she did. She won't be there tonight. She has to work this weekend."

I followed John's lead through most of my life. He would get a job and I joined him, with very good results. That began to change just before I entered high school. John applied for a position at Bailey's, a downtown department store. Before they accepted him, he got a better paying job in a factory. At Dad's insistence, I actually assumed John's identity and became Bailey's new stock boy.

Trying to remember that I was John became extremely stressful. They must have thought they had hired the village idiot when they called me. It usually took three or four shouts of "John" before I remembered that they were talking to me. The job did have many benefits, especially when I started to date Jackie, a fellow clerk at Bailey's. She was three years older than me. It became even trickier trying to maintain John's identity while on a date. Of course, I could not introduce her to any of my friends. That would surely blow my cover.

In my sophomore year in high school, John and a group of our friends formed a car club called *The Barons*. We were the royalty of the high school set, if only in our own minds. Though I was one of the youngest members of the group, I became their president. I seemed to be willing to follow through with the ideas the group originated. John never seemed to resent this, but now he was once again assuming the role as my leader.

John and I went to Tokyo alone. He did not invite any of the other Airmen from his barracks.

"My routine is like that of a milkman. I stop at the same bars in the same order each time I go into town. They know me and know when to expect me to stop by." "We'll start at the FEAF Club." The lobby of that Club had a grand curving stairway right out of a Fred Astaire and Ginger Rogers movie. We climbed that stairway to a fine nightclub with waiters in uniform wearing white gloves.

"I usually start with a drink or two here," John explained. "Everything is so inexpensive, but only the best. I'll take a Canadian Club and ginger ale," he ordered when the waiter approached us.

"Make mine the same."

"From here we'll go to the Tokyo Onsen," John explained while we sipped our drinks. "Onsen means 'hot springs'. We can get a massage there," he said without asking if I was interested. After a couple of drinks we took a taxi to a two-story building.

"They give massages on the top floor. That's where we'll start," he announced.

"We would like to get a massage," John said to the receptionist in Japanese giving her our names. John led the way into the bar where we had a drink while waiting our turn.

"You'll love the Japanese beer called Kirin," he said ordering one for each of us. John had written in his letters about the Japanese beer and how he could drink it by the quart. This did not seem likely, as he never could hold more than two beers in a night. The beer proved to be delicious.

"I have to take a leak," John said as we finished our first quart.

"Me, too."

While standing at a bank of urinals, somebody startled me with a tap on the shoulder. They said something in Japanese. On turning, I was even more stunned to find a lovely Japanese lady standing there in panties and bra - a pretty young thing - and in the men's room. Without even turning, John said something to her in her native tongue and she left without saying another word.

"What did she want?" I sputtered.

"She wanted to know if you were Mr. Johnson. Apparently he is next to get a massage."

"Why ask me and not you?"

"The power of the uniform probably attracted her. Maybe she assumed you were a person of authority. They don't see military uniforms in this part of Tokyo, especially sailors. In fact, most branches of the service don't wear their uniforms off base."

"She just comes into the men's room?" I asked incredulously.

"They don't think anything of that here in Japan."

I was soon to learn much more about Japanese customs. During our rub down, hot and cold showers, all jointly performed by young ladies, I became sexually aroused. They giggled. After our massages, we proceeded down to the main floor.

"This is a large community swimming pool, which the Japanese call a bathhouse," John continued his tour. I was stunned to find families; men, women and children, all swimming in the nude.

"Is it normal for all the people to be naked?"

"Yes, but don't worry. We're not going swimming. I just wanted you to see the place." We watched for a while so that I could take it all in before we moved on.

"Now we'll go to a dancehall which is located on the Ginza, the Broadway of Tokyo," John said as he hailed another taxicab. "Wait until you see this place." John's expensive taste, not only included tailor-made suits, but he took taxicabs rather than the cheaper rickshaws.

The dancehall was a grand ballroom filled with hostesses dressed in formal gowns. It looked like a movie set with more than a hundred petite young ladies, each one lovelier than the next.

"The hostesses are hired to meet and greet the businessmen who frequent this place. They dance with anyone wishing to waltz across the floor." The place held hundreds of people. The orchestra played American *big band* dance music popular in the States before and during World War II. The wooden paneling on the walls looked expensive.

"We'll sit and watch from here," John said as he selected an empty table. Hostesses arrived immediately. John spoke to them in Japanese. They took a seat, one on either side of me. I tried to turn on my charm, but they could not understand a word I said.

As I scoped out the rest of the room I said, "Look at that balcony circling the entire dance floor."

"That's so people can sit and watch the dancers and hostesses. Oh my God," John said suddenly pointing at some Japanese fellows harassing an American. "That guy is from my barracks and he's in big trouble. Stay here and sit tight," he said as he sped away.

The next thing I knew John was back with his friend from the balcony and four young Japanese fellows. They looked like hoodlums I had seen in American "B" movies. They were still not happy with John's Air Force buddy, Roy, but John seemed to be able to restrain them. It was then that I realized they were all dressed exactly like John, including the same style haircut, a *ducktail*. John looked like he was one of their gang. Indeed, not only did they treat him as one of them, they acted as if John was royalty.

No sooner had John gotten everyone settled at the table when the ladies got all excited and started to flutter. Their attention was focused on the entrance of the dance hall. A young man standing at the front door was surrounded by a group of young ladies. They looked like his entourage. He too, was dressed in a dark blue suit, white shirt, and dark tie. His hair had the well-oiled look of our new-found friends, but it was cut shorter. From the reaction of the hostesses we knew he was a man of importance.

"What's that all about?" I asked John.

"Wait a second. I'll find out," and off John went. He struck up a conversation with the young man. The entourage turned and headed for our table. Our newfound friends were amazed by John's power over people. They showed their respect by bringing more chairs for our guests and ordering drinks for all. Before I knew it, we were surrounded by a throng of hostesses.

"This guy is a famous actor from a hot, running play on the Ginza," John explained to me when he got a free moment. The hoodlums were buying drinks faster than we could consume them. We were just one big happy family!

Suddenly, the star stood up, said something to John and bowed. John stood and bowed to him. The star left the hall followed by his entourage. Most of the hostesses followed him to the door. In the commotion, one of the hoodlums spilled a drink on one of the others. The guy leapt to his feet screaming and waving his arms in the air.

This is it! We are going to have a brawl, I thought. I sprang to my feet and got a firm hold on the back of my chair. I didn't know if I needed it as a weapon or a shield. Their leader said something that quieted the group down instantly. He pulled out a thick wad of money and peeled off a few bills, which he shoved at a third member of the group. The third guy took the money and left the table. *How this was going to solve anything is a mystery to me, but everyone else was satisfied.*

"What's going on?" I asked John. "Everything happened so fast I didn't understand what they were saying." It was at this point that I figured out that our new friends were not hoodlums. *Anybody with that much cash must be gangsters, like in Chicago during the 1930s,* I thought

The people at our table settled down and went back to drinking while John talked to their leader. John had some kind of magical hold over this guy. As long as the leader was happy the gang was too. The ladies drifted back to our table. Drinks continued to flow, all paid for by our new friends. The third gangster returned carrying three new dress shirts still in their wrappers. The guy with the wet shirt stood up, looked at all three then selected one of them. He took off his jacket, then his shirt which he threw onto the floor. He then put on the chosen shirt. Everyone seemed pleased. John continued his conversation with their leader, as everything returned to normal.

John said after a while, "Let's blow this pop stand." After saying something to the leader of the gang, John stood up and bowed to him. The leader stood up, responded and bowed to John.

Each of the members of the gang took turns bowing to John. Indeed, John was the *Baron of Tokyo*.

As we left the hall John said, "I love it here. I would stay in the Air Force for twenty years if they let me spend it here in Japan."

"Not me!" said Roy, John's buddy. "I would leave Japan tomorrow if they let me. Right now I'm going back to the safety of my barracks."

John and I continued our tour of Tokyo's nightlife. Our last stop was a nightclub called Maxim's.

"This place is a clone of the famous nightclub in Paris, France, by the same name," John told me. Everywhere we went John knew the bartenders. He had quite a following of both men and women, all Japanese. Maxim's was no exception. "Take a look at the restroom," John insisted after ordering drinks for us. The men's room looked like an expensive one I had seen once in a downtown Cleveland hotel. Rich wooden panels, wood counters with shiny sinks and fixtures, subtle lighting presented a luxurious appearance. Then I spotted an elegantly dressed Western woman in an evening gown looking into the mirror, fixing her makeup. She took one look at me and fled almost knocking John down as he came through the door.

"I saw her come in here while we were ordering drinks. I didn't think she knew that in Japan the restrooms are co-ed," John chuckled. "That's why I wanted you to come in here."

When we closed Maxim's that night, we were very happy and feeling no pain. John hailed a taxicab for our ride back to the barracks.

"Wouldn't it be great fun if we drove?" John said. He loved to drive, but John had not been behind the wheel of a car in more than a year. It didn't take much persuading to get the driver to relinquish the wheel, just a stack of money. We sat in the front seat, John at the wheel. The driver got into the back. John had a difficult time remembering that the Japanese drive on the left side of the road. At one point, we passed an oncoming car on the wrong side. Horns blared; we waved and continued on our way. Our driver laughed nervously. We ended up back at the barracks all in one piece.

Yokosuka

Back at our ship, docked at Yokosuka, Japan, the guys in Fire Control eagerly offered to introduce me to this foreign land. They went on their first liberty without me, not realizing the rich Japanese culture I had already experienced in Tokyo, in ways they never would. I did not spoil their fun with stories of my adventures with my brother John, the *Baron of Tokyo.*

Max Gilmore, a southern Indiana farm boy, took us to his favorite bar in Yokosuka. We filed into a large dark room lit with lanterns, which looked more like a social club than a bar. The place was nearly empty, so we easily found a table big enough to hold our gang. Seating ourselves, we scoped out the place. The walls were splendidly decorated with a motif of dragons, mountain scenes, and women in kimonos, gathering around some point of interest. The Japanese kimonos were elaborately embroidered silk or satin gowns with long, full sleeves. A wide sash, called an obi, usually in a contrasting color, accentuated the kimonos. The ladies wore high collars that stood up behind the neck. Their elegantly coiffured hair was held in a tight upsweep bun with oriental combs. White foundation makeup covered each lady's entire face, highlighted with precise eyeliner, eyebrows and accentuated lips. They wore soft slippers on their feet.

No sooner had we gotten situated at our table when women surrounded us. I was expecting women dressed in the traditional kimonos like on the walls. But these women wore long form fitting brocaded sheath dresses of vivid hues of red, green, blue, and gold, with provocative slits up either side of the dress. Their Mandarin collars, frog corded closures and dramatic eyeliner added to their look. They reminded me of the waitresses in the Chinese restaurants our family frequented in my youth with the exception that their hair was cut short in the Hollywood style of the day. These ladies wore wooden platform sandals on their feet.

"The ladies are here to entertain us," Max pointed out. We scrambled for chairs to accommodate the new arrivals, one for each of us. We sailors ordered our favorite Nipponese beer and turned to the young ladies to see what they wanted. They wanted to talk to us or should I say, listen.

The woman next to me asked in very good, if accented English, "Whele ale you flom?"

"The *John W Weeks*," I told her after figuring out what she had said. "It is a destroyer of the United States Navy," I continued. She listened very attentively—hanging on my every word.

"She knows what ship you are on," Max informed me. "These ladies have better intelligence info than the U.S. Navy. If you ask her where the *Weeks'* next port of call is, she can tell you. Try asking her."

"Where is the *Weeks* going when it leaves Yokosuka?"

"Sasebo," she answered without elaborating.

"I didn't know that!" I said to Max in astonishment.

"They know everything. They have a network of ladies all over the city. Those ladies talk to Navy guys at all levels. Then the ladies compare notes. The Navy should be so lucky to have such an intelligence network."

"By the way, when she asked you where are you from she wanted to know something new, like where were you born."

"Ohio?" I told her.

"*Ohio, gasiamos,*" she giggled as she bowed.

"That means good morning in Japanese," Max explained to me. "She thought you were trying to greet her in her native tongue. If you were you should have said, *Kombonwa*, which means, 'Good evening'. He is from Cleveland, Ohio," Max explained to her.

"Oh," she said putting her hand to her mouth as she giggled again.

"What is your name?" I asked her.

"My name is Koseko." I noticed these women were all beautiful, animated, and very friendly.

"Hello, Koseko. My name is Mark."

"Malk," she repeated several times probably trying to memorize it. "Malk, how wong have you been in ze Navy," she asked and then listened to the story of my life with all the interest of watching a movie unfold. That gave me an idea.

"Do you like movies, Koseko?"

"Oh, yes!" she said and rattled off a list of American movies she had seen.

"Who is your favorite actress?" I asked.

"Audley Hebbuln," she answered without having to think.

"Who?" I could not translate the name.

"Audley Hebbuln," she repeated. I puzzled over that without asking again not wanting to embarrass her. She was so adorable.

"Who is your favorite actor?" I asked.

"Glegoly Beck." she answered without hesitation.

"Who?"

"Glegoly Beck." she said again. Realizing I did not understand her she said, "Glegoly Beck in Loman Horiday wiz Audley Hebbuln."

Now I was really confused. "Max, I need a translator here." Once I had Max's attention, I asked her to repeat the name of her favorite movie star one more time.

"Glegoly Beck in Loman Horiday wiz Audley Hebbuln." she said again without getting frustrated. Max's face screwed up into a questioning look as he stroked his beard in contemplation. She repeated it again, slower this time. His face lit up in recognition.

"She likes Gregory Peck in *Roman Holiday* with Audrey Hepburn."

"Sameo, sameo," I answered meaning I agreed with her. "He is great! I have not seen Roman Holiday yet." *Who is Audrey Hepburn*, I thought to myself as I ordered another round of drinks.

Suddenly there was a scream from across the room.

"Moxy, Moxy." We turned to see what was happening. A beautiful woman shuffled towards Max. "Moxy," she screamed again getting closer. This behavior was definitely not normal for Japanese women. They were normally rather reserved, trying not to display emotions. Max rose to his feet in astonishment.

"Michiko," he screamed as he rushed into her arms.

"How did you get hele?" she asked apparently never expecting to see him again.

"I told you I would return," Max said giving her a great big hug as he swept her off her feet swinging her in a big circle. Her sandals flew across the room. One of the other ladies scurried across the room to retrieve them. After assisting with her footwear, Max brought his friend to our table.

"This is my geisha girl. Remember me telling you about her?" After introducing Michiko to each of us individually they moved off to a table in a corner alone.

"Can you believe Max came all the way around the world to see Michiko again?" I asked Koseko.

"Cool, da nah," she answered, meaning "Cool, don't you think." *Well that translated easily,* I thought. *Can it really be Japanese?*

"Do you think the same will happen to us, Koseko?"

"Rots of ruck," she said cheerfully. Meaning, lots of luck. *Yeah, I guess you are right*, I thought to myself. *I may never even return to this bar let alone find you here.*

"Do you come here often or do you go to a different bar every night?"

"Sameo, sameo," she said. "I wolk hele." I realized this to mean, I work here. I was catching on to their version of English.

Max Gilmore's legend began that night. Back at the ship we told everyone about the gorgeous woman who loves Max and had been waiting more than a year for his return. From that day on, we called him Moxy.

68.
Visions and Memories of Loved Ones
Renee Batenjany

Do not be afraid, bodies will come and go but visions and memories of our loved ones will remain stained in our minds.

Seize the memories friend of mine and hold them close to your heart

and mind, so you may recall those special and dear moments from time to time.

Fear not my friend, for our loved ones are at rest, traveling to the

Grand Place to meet our "Mighty Lord".

Remember this friend, our loved ones are now special angels traveling at your side to help guide you through the mystery of life.

69.
What's NEXT?
(formerly known as BASCC)
Sara Burnside

I like it! ...the new name of our Birmingham Senior Center. It connotes a positive step forward. Whether you are persons of the ages fifty through ninety, you are moving through stages in life and need to consider what is next. Perhaps a retirement, job loss, divorce, empty nest or just a need for something different can cause you to change direction. My ninety-seven-year-old aunt needed to move to assisted living, my niece sent her two kids to college, and a friend was ready to retire. Each needed to consider how they would spend the now available time.

An adjective or adverb, the word "next" provokes excitement. It suggests a place where one could explore, discuss, learn, move, or just enjoy the company of like-minded age-mates.

As their brochure full of activities and events to look forward to notes: NEXT embraces a New Look; New Attitude; and a New Name. Come see what's next for you!

70.
Why I Write
Sara Burnside

President Barrack Obama responded in a Time Magazine interview (December 31 issue) that the reason he keeps a diary is to clarify what he believes, what he sees, what he cares about and deeply held values. He also finds that writing is a process for him to convert a jumble of thoughts into coherent sentences and to challenge himself with tough questions. In this interview, President Obama also related how President Abraham Lincoln's writing had progressed from that of a young lawyer to the maturity and wisdom of the Gettysburg Address. Through the process of his writing, he was able to take very conflicting forces and opinions of the times and turn them into a universal version of what our country is and should be.

For an ordinary person like me, the reasons above are the same. Writing in my journal allows me to express sometimes very strong feelings, opinions, and ideas. And similarly, I find I am figuring out all of these thoughts as I write. For many authors, whether published or not, their writing is a permanent legacy of their life stories and events that can be shared with family and friends.

We writers and authors of NEXT's Writers' Corner invite everyone who likes to write or are curious about what we do, to join us on the first and third Thursdays of the month. We have poems, life story writers, journalists, and always listeners as members; Join us!

71.
Woman Driver
Al Rosie

This works much better when done to Frederick Loewe's music to "Guinevere"
from "Camelot".

From the garage, down the drive
Will I get back alive?
Trepidation's what I feel
When my wife is at the wheel.

As my heart skips a beat
She backs into the street
Looking neither left nor right
Is another car in sight?

Oh, the wild screech it makes
As he slams on the brakes
While she blithely drives away
It's no wonder I've turned gray.

Now my gut starts to churn
For she's making a turn
Can you guess why I'm up tight?
From the left lane, she turns right.

On the freeway we go
And she's driving quite slow
While I plead with her in vain
Let's get out of the fast lane.

Now, it gets even worse
For she opens her purse
While the guy just behind's
Going out of his mind.

As I'm quaking with terror
She applies her mascara
And I'm thinking we should break up
What a time to fix her makeup.

Oh my God this is hell
For she's dialing her cell
And you know what comes next
Yes, she's starting to text!

By a miracle of salvation
We achieve our destination
 So it's time to end this poem
Bet your booty, I DRIVE HOME!

72.
Women in the World
Sara Burnside

Even as a shy teenager, diaries were my outlet for my thoughts, ideas, and fears. Now as a not-so-young woman, journals still serve as a record of my life and issues I feel strongly about. Recently I saw a PBS "Front Line" documentary about how women are treated around the world, and the solutions that counter the abuse and violence against women. Thus, I would like to share my reactions to this issue of Women in the World.

Unfortunately, as a Christian woman myself, religion is often the reason women are abused and treated as less-valued in society. In Somalia, female circumcision is practiced to assure girls will not express their sexuality. In Kenya, young girls are sold, even by their impoverished parents, to the sex trade. Even in our Detroit area, a young woman was killed because her father was angered by her "wild behavior."

Lest we think that such treatment toward women only happens in primitive societies, it was not so long ago that women were considered second-class citizens in America. Deprived of the right to vote and not defended in case of rape or domestic abuse, women were forced to fight for their rights as American citizens.

The happy news is that many non-profit groups and Hollywood stars (e.g. George Clooney) are taking on this issue. By providing low-interest loans, these groups are providing women around the world opportunities to start small businesses. With economic independence, women no longer are stuck with abusive husbands.

And by becoming "bread winners" in families, women are feeling a new-found confidence and power over their own destinies. Women have intrinsic value as the Mother of new life and as children of God, and now they are beginning to get the respect in society that they deserve.

73.
Yak, Rapid River
Renee Batenjany

Wet, wild, crazy, and funny Yak River you are!

Begging six innocent campers and others to take the grand challenge of rafting the Pennsylvania waters.

Calling us to take the rubber boat and plunge into the heavy rocky waters!

Paddle, paddle, paddle, reverse paddle, "you sing out, "ouch" into the rocks, and out of the spinning cess-pool waters!

Drifting down the rough waters, turning over many times, drinking the river water, and latching on to rocks, tree branches like ropes with hopes of reaching calm waters!

Oh, what adventures of unyielding, exciting and unusual risk of venue you have stirred within us "calling for more!"

Contributing Authors

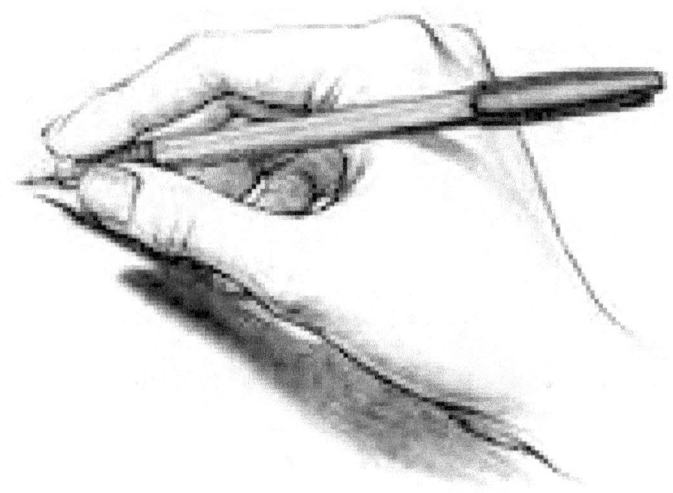

Al Rosie

Al Rosie

Where are you from?

Birmingham, Michigan; by way of Chicago, Cicero and Detroit.

When and why did you begin writing?

I began writing at age forty-seven, writing lyrics for appearances on local Gong Shows. I was gonged in twenty-three out of thirty appearances.

What would you say is your most interesting writing quirk?

I type with two fingers.

What do you like to do when you're not writing?

I play bridge, bowl, play golf, babysit, and fish.

As a child, what did you want to do when you grew up?

I wanted to remain a child; and so far, I've succeeded fairly well.

B. Silver

B. Silver

Where are you from?

Canada, a big place. Good area, too (comment attributed to Jim Price, Detroit Tigers Radio Broadcast Co-host, with Dan Dickerson.) He always says, "good area" when talking about a location, a city.

When and why did you begin writing?

Second grade. The first word I remember learning? It was 'wagon'. I saw two words in that one word. 'Wag' and 'on.' That's how I learned to speak a word and to spell it. By separating it into parts. Then I could make the whole word and I'd remember it better that way, to say it and spell it. Words became different kind of communicating 'tools', just by watching the comedians on The Ed Sullivan Show. Norm Crosby, Jack Carter, Red Sklelton, and Sid Cesar. They were special because they knew how to use words.

What would you say is your most interesting writing quirk?

Never being serious. Always finding the funny way through a word. Using words to convey the unexpected. Words are tools, aren't they? Making words into pictures, creating images in one's mind, to make people laugh. Looking at something and changing it, with words.

What do you like to do when you're not writing?

Think. It gets me to write some more.

As a child, what did you want to do when you grew up?

To still be in Grade 8-A. Mr. Chesney was the English teacher. We learned a couple of Polish words in his English class. He was extending our understanding of words, using words of different languages that convey the same thing for every person, everywhere. He was a good teacher. I remember him. Dziekuje, Mr. Chesney.

Celia P. Ransom

Celia P. Ransom

Where are you from?

I am from a small town in Michigan.

When and why did you begin writing?

I have always written. For many years, I simply wrote letters to family and friends. Around 2005, I began writing poems for friends, and my grandchildren. I went through a low point in my life and the writing was a distraction. It took a while, however, to share with others who were not close to me.

What would you say is your most interesting writing quirk?

I keep pen and paper by the bed, as I often awake in the night with lines of a poem or story going through my head I have to write it down before returning to rest.

What do you like to do when you're not writing?

I read. I love well-written and well-acted movies. I love spending time with family and friends at our cottage in northern Michigan. I also love chatting on the phone with those close to me.

As a child, what did you want to do when you grew up?

I wanted to be in the movies. I think I still do, but would probably be terrified now.

Dee Trainor

Dee Trainor

Where are you from?

I was born in Birmingham, Michigan.

When and why did you begin writing?

I started to write about six years ago. I have always been the "story-teller" of our family, and my family and friends encouraged me to put my stories on paper.

What would you say is your most interesting writing quirk?

I always write long-hand.

What do you like to do when you're not writing?

I am an artist and have been painting for more than twenty-five years. I also have a large family who I am very close to, and I am constantly on the go, keeping busy.

As a child, what did you want to do when you grew up?

As a child, I wanted to either be a newspaper reporter or a lady detective.

Diana Kathryn Plopa

Diana Kathryn Plopa

Where are you from?

I was born in Seattle, Washington. We moved to Michigan when I was four, and I lived in Boston, Massachusetts for three years in my early twenties. I still think of myself, at least in my creative soul, as a displaced Bostonian; I love that place!

When and why did you begin writing?

I've been writing since my father taught me how to hold a crayon. Words have always fascinated me. I think I wrote my first real story in First Grade. I remember that a duck was the main character.

What would you say is your most interesting writing quirk?

I type 120 words per minute, and often feel gently schizophrenic, as I take dictation and transcribe meetings and conversations between my characters.

What do you like to do when you're not writing?

I love to kayak, hike, ride horses, swim, read, sail, hang out with my writing buddies, and play miniature golf.

As a child, what did you want to do when you grew up?

I had my heart set on being a veterinarian until I discovered how much math was involved. After that, my heart and soul were dedicated to writing – but I had to accept a few "real jobs" along the way while raising my son. Now, I'm completely consumed by words; writing my own books and helping others to publish their work.

Diane Bert, Ph.D.

Dora Saber

Dora Saber

Where are you from?

Lebanon.

When and why did you begin writing?

Two years ago. I have a few interesting incidents in life which I wanted to share with my family, friends, and relatives.

What would you say is your most interesting writing quirk?

Nothing special.

What do you like to do when you're not writing?

I like to read and do puzzles.

As a child, what did you want to do when you grew up?

I wanted to be a pharmacist.

Jerry McKeon

Where are you from?

Born and raised in Flint, Michigan. I lived in the north end of the city – mostly factory workers. I went to a Private Catholic School mostly attend by Polish and Slovak families living in the area. Half of my class knew how to play the accordion.

When and why did you begin writing?

I've written all my life. At work I wrote press releases, for fun, I wrote limericks. My grandfather has a whole book of poems he wrote over his lifetime. I guess I got my gift of writing from him. I've published a book of poetry and I have some seller assistance pamphlets copyrighted – they were used in my former real estate practice.

What would you say is your most interesting writing quirk?

I often try to inject humor in my writings. My poems usually tell a story.

What do you like to do when you're not writing?

I work out five to six days a week in the gym. I used to bike a lot until a serious accident curtailed it. I drive a 100-year-old man to his office every day.

As a child, what did you want to do when you grew up?

A manager of a hotel. In my early twenties, I did land a job as manager of a Howard Johnson Motel but after a visit by a large group of Roller Derby Girls. I changed my mind – they wrecked the place.

Mark A. Kelly

Mark A. Kelly

Where are you from?

I was born and raised in northern Ohio. After graduating from the University of Dayton as an engineer, I eventually moved to Detroit in 1965.

When and why did you begin writing?

One of my college professors suggested that I should write the story of my life. I finally got around to writing several books.

What would you say is your most interesting writing quirk?

I love to write dialogue.

What do you like to do when you're not writing?

I try to sell my books.

As a child, what did you want to do when you grew up?

I had no idea what I wanted to do when I grew up. I was too busy working. My first job was taking tickets at a Dancehall at age ten.

.

Niru Prasad

Niru Prasad

Where are you from?

India.

When and why did you begin writing?

Writing has always been my passion and I started writing since I was a teenager.

What would you say is your most interesting writing quirk?

I would like to teach our youngsters to study hard, stay focused and help their community.

What do you like to do when you're not writing?

I am a busy physician, housewife, mother and grandmother. I like to perform my duties in life.

As a child, what did you want to do when you grew up?

I always wanted to become a doctor so I could help others in whichever way I can.

Renee Batenjany

Where are you from?

I grew up in Detroit, Michigan. I moved with my family to Beverly Hills, Michigan and am now living a pleasant walk from Birmingham, Michigan.

When and why did you begin writing?

I am inspired by others; my feelings and emotions.

What would you say is your most interesting writing quirk?

I write Thank You notes for Christmas. I write about friends and coworkers; and special moments others have shared with me.

What do you like to do when you're not writing?

I enjoy walking in parks, malls, etc. I enjoy creative drawing and rendering with colored markers. I enjoy traveling with groups by bus, car, and checking out miscellaneous retail, rummage and garage sales. I enjoy exercising, eating out, and light, funny movies.

As a child, what did you want to do when you grew up?

I wanted to get a full-time job and move out, buy my own house, get a car, get married and have a few fun children. I had dreams of becoming a dentist, artist, or perhaps start a local corner store with an ice cream counter.

Sara Burnside

Sara Burnside

Where are you from?

I was born in a small Ohio town where everyone knew you and followed your growth from birth to college, and maybe beyond.

When and why did you begin writing?

I always kept diaries as a young girl; wrote letters to my parents about my experiences as a traveling teacher; and since have filled several journals with my thoughts and opinions regarding my life, politics, and world events.

What would you say is your most interesting writing quirk?

That I don't want editing or others' opinions!

What do you like to do when you're not writing?

I keep busy with church activities, NEXT classes, and time with my friends and family.

As a child, what did you want to do when you grew up?

My mom strongly led me in the direction of teaching, which I did and loved.

Shelia Becker

Shelia Becker

Where are you from?

Millstreet, County Cork, Ireland.

When and why did you begin writing?

In my fifties; and to tell my story and the story of others.

What would you say is your most interesting writing quirk?

Detail, detail, detail.

What do you like to do when you're not writing?

Telling stories.

As a child, what did you want to do when you grew up?

To get away from oppressive Ireland. My nursing degree was my ticket to America.

Shirley Gach

Shirley Gach

Where are you from?

I was born in Detroit, Michigan. I now live in Birmingham, Michigan.

When and why did you begin writing?

I fell in love with writing while taking a creative writing class in college. Also, I liked writing a monthly column for The American Women's Club (Germany) on environmental issues. The latter gave me a platform to share information and ideas.

What would you say is your most interesting writing quirk?

I don't think I have one.

What do you like to do when you're not writing?

I enjoy photography, watercolor painting, hanging out with my grandchildren and photographing my grandchildren.

As a child, what did you want to do when you grew up?

Attend art school; be a teacher.

Susanne Sack

Susanne Sack

Where are you from?

I was born in Detroit, Michigan and was educated mostly in Detroit. I graduated from Wayne State University in 1961 in special education speech therapy. I worked in Detroit schools for a short time until my husband and I moved to Europe for two years. We returned to Southfield, Michigan.

When and why did you begin writing?

As a child, I started writing at home when I found writing to be fun. I had a newspaper for the family and wrote fairy tales and thought about writing plays. I think I was about eleven when I got interested in books and writing.

What would you say is your most interesting writing quirk?

I believe my imagination helps me create a world for my readers.

What do you like to do when you're not writing?

I play and practice my piano. I have written music, a musical play. My husband and I like to visit our children in four different states. We have traveled in Europe and other places inside and outside the USA.

As a child, what did you want to do when you grew up?

I liked to play and not work. At eight years old, I thought I'd love to be a stage director; but my people skills prevented that, or so I thought. So I became a teacher and a mom, which happens to be a form of stage directing.

www.ingramcontent.com/pod-product-compliance
Lightning Source LLC
Chambersburg PA
CBHW070845250626
47159CB00003B/935